NOWHERE TO HIDE

J.P. BOWIE

Nowhere to Hide
ISBN # 978-0-85715-423-1
©Copyright J.P.Bowie 2011
Cover Art by April Martinez ©Copyright 2011
Interior text design by Claire Siemaszkiewicz
Total-E-Bound Publishing

Published in 2011 by Total-E-Bound Publishing, Think Tank, Ruston Way, Lincoln, LN6 7FL, United Kingdom.

NOWHERE TO HIDE

Dedication

Claire, my thanks for your skillful editing and support,
and for Phil - Always

Chapter One

Darfur: A territory of the Sudan

The heat outside the makeshift emergency clinic was close to unbearable. Doctor Mark Hamilton wiped the sweat from his forehead and took a long swig from the bottle of water he carried. Northern Darfur was not, and never would be, the ideal spot for a summer vacation, he mused, with a wry twist to his generous mouth. Not for the first time he wondered who he should thank at 'Doctors who Care International' for sending him to this cosy spot.

"Dr. Hamilton?"

Mark turned at the sound of one of the nurses calling to him from inside the tent that served as a refugee camp emergency clinic until the promised, more permanent hospital was built. *Promises, promises.* Mark had tired of officialdom's lack of coming through on those promises, and had more or less resigned himself to looking after his patients as best he could, with what medical supplies he'd brought with him, and what the UN sent sporadically.

"What is it, Asima?"

The pretty young nurse gazed up at Mark from dark eyes, rimmed with tiredness. "It is Ghali, Doctor. His breathing is strange again."

Mark sighed. Ghali, a young boy, had been brought to the clinic two days earlier suffering from dehydration and borderline malnutrition. Not an uncommon malady in this part of the world, but the boy had been wearing clothes that told Mark Ghali was not one of the thousands of poor, undernourished children living in Northern Darfur. His shirt and shorts were of good quality, his shoes more than serviceable. The few words he'd uttered since he'd been brought in by the goat herder who'd found him lying among some rocks were not of the local dialect. Mark's guess was that he did not come from any nearby town or village, which led to the inevitable questions—what on earth was he doing here, miles from home, and how had he managed to get this far?

So far, Ghali had not answered either of those questions. He'd simply gazed up at Mark with eyes like fathomless dark pools of sadness. Something bad had happened to the boy, and he was either too ashamed or too traumatised to tell anyone of it.

Mark followed Asima into the clinic, and walked between the long line of beds that flanked either side of the narrow canvassed structure. As usual, Ghali stared at Mark as he approached the bed, his eyes wary, as if he expected Mark to pick him up and throw him outside.

"*Salam*, Ghali. *Kaifa haloka* – how are you?" The boy visibly flinched when Mark knelt by the bedside and placed a hand on his forehead.

"He does not seem to understand," Asima said quietly.

"Could be my lousy Arabic. Easy there, kid," Mark murmured. "No one here is going to hurt you." He brushed back the black curly hair from Ghali's brow. He took the thermometer Asima handed him and pushed it gently into the boy's ear. "His temperature is slightly elevated, but nothing to worry about," he told Asima after glancing at the reading. "His rapid breathing is a product of his nervousness. He doesn't trust us yet."

Mark was loath to give Ghali a sedative. He was desperately low on that kind of medication and preferred to keep it for those patients with painful wounds suffered in rebel attacks. Every day he and the nurses treated victims of shootings or torture at the hands of the rebel factions that were rampant in Darfur. Still, he would like Ghali to have a peaceful night. He knew the boy had spent both nights at the clinic unable to sleep, his eyes wide open as if afraid to close them for fear of something, or someone, lurking nearby.

Mark stood, ready to go to his own quarters and get a sleeping pill for Ghali. *Half a pill would probably do...* He stopped, surprised, when a small hand slid into his. Ghali looked up at him, his dark eyes glistening with unshed tears. Mark knelt by his side again, and gently squeezed the boy's hand.

"You'll be all right," he murmured in his halting Arabic, wishing he'd spent more time on this difficult language. "You're safe here."

Ghali slowly shook his head, then said a few words more clearly but in a language that had Mark at a loss. He looked at Asima helplessly.

"I think that he is speaking Turkish," Asima explained. "I understand a little. He says something about bad men looking for him."

"Tell him there are no bad men here."

Before Asima could speak, Ghali said in English, "They will come. They look for me. They will never give up…my family…"

A shiver of dread ran down Mark's spine at the boy's words. The last thing he needed was for a gang of cutthroats to terrorise the already fragile psyches of his patients, not to mention the nurses. He might yet be glad of the gun he had hidden in his medical bag, back at his quarters. He knew he couldn't rely on the government security force that patrolled the area in a desultory, and sometimes hostile, manner. He'd already had quite a few run-ins with the so-called patrol commander, an arrogant idiot named Dhul Fiqar, who claimed to be of royal descent and considered Mark, along with the nurses and patients, less than worthy of his concern. He treated Mark with a certain disdain, but the young doctor was only too aware of the long looks Fiqar would throw his way. Looks that if they could, Mark swore would bore under his clothes and strip him naked. He had an inkling Fiqar would like nothing better than to see the 'American doctor' humiliated at his hands.

He squeezed Ghali's hand again. "You are safe here," he repeated. If he couldn't set the boy's mind at ease, he at least could guarantee him a good night's rest. "I'll get him a sleeping pill," he told Asima. "Give it to him a half-hour before lights-out."

As Mark walked through the blistering heat to the tent he'd called 'home' for the past three months since he'd arrived in Darfur, he heard the low thrum of an engine high above him. He looked up to see a helicopter circling overhead. *Probably a patrol looking for rebels*, he thought grimly. Last time a government helicopter had landed near the clinic they'd come on the misinformation that rebels were being hidden by Mark inside the clinic. It had taken Mark most of the day to convince the soldiers they were mistaken, even after they'd searched the clinic and found only terrified patients, and no rebels hiding under the beds.

Peering upwards, he tried to make out the markings on the side of the helicopter. Something unfamiliar…and that caused another shiver down his spine at the thought it might just be the men Ghali had mentioned were looking for him. He quickened his pace. There wasn't much he alone could do, even with a gun in his hand, but if the men meant trouble, they would at least see he wasn't going to stand for them abducting a young defenceless boy from his care. Inside his tent, he rummaged through his medical bag until he felt the warm metal of the gun's handle. He pulled the Browning SFS, a gift from his father, from his bag and hefted it in his hand, then checked the clip. Okay. He hadn't a clue what he'd do if this turned into a nasty confrontation. He'd never actually fired the gun except in a firing range, and he'd never even contemplated shooting a *person* — but they weren't going to take Ghali if he could prevent it. He stepped out of his tent and stared at the helicopter as it slowly circled once more, then prepared to land.

Oh, boy…

He watched it touch down like an awkward bird attempting its first landing. Two men jumped out, then turned to help a third man out of the 'copter. Mark frowned. The man was obviously injured. He was bare-chested and Mark could see blood on his shoulder and arm. He stuck the gun under his belt and walked towards the men.

"You the doctor?" one of them yelled over the noise of the 'copter blades.

"Yes," Mark yelled back.

As they drew closer Mark could see the one who had asked was tall and ruggedly good looking with close cropped dark hair. He stared at Mark from thickly lashed, ice-blue eyes. Eyes that didn't miss the gun Mark was carrying.

"Got a wounded man here. Took a bullet in the shoulder. Can you help?"

For a moment, Mark's step faltered. *This guy is gorgeous.* The soldier wore a dark green sleeveless shirt and Mark found he couldn't take his eyes off the man's smoothly muscled arms, or the dusting of chest hair the scooped neck of the shirt revealed. *Pull yourself together, idiot...*

"Of course," Mark said, his voice unsteady. "Bring him over to the clinic."

"Thanks." Mark fell into step beside the man who held out a big hand. "Sergeant Major Caruthers..." He shook Mark's hand in a solid tingling grip. "Some call me Boomer. Our walking wounded here is Private Paddy O'Brien, and that's Warrant Officer Harry Mathers." He indicated the man on the other side of O'Brien with a side flick of his head.

Mark nodded at the men. "Doctor Hamilton." He wondered at the man's accent. "You guys Marines?"

"Diggers—Australian Army, Special Ops. We're part of the UN's peace keeping force."

Mark guided them into the clinic and called Asima over. "We're going to have to operate to remove a bullet," he told her. "I'll need a local anaesthetic." He turned to Caruthers. "Lay him down here on the table so I can take a proper look."

"You expecting trouble?" the officer asked, indicating Mark's gun, still under his belt.

"Oh…this. I didn't recognise the markings on the 'copter, and we've had some problems here in the past."

"Don't know a kangaroo when you see one?" He gave Mark a lopsided grin and a wink.

"Uh, well, yeah…" Mark grinned back. "Just not on a chopper before."

"We would've taken him to the hospital in Al Fashir, but this place was closer, and we figured he needed this taken care of ASAP."

"How did this happen?"

"Rebels. We'd just dropped off food supplies to a village north of here, when they hit us. Bastards were hiding in one of the huts."

Mark turned his attention to the wounded man. The young Australian looked up at Mark through pain-filled eyes. "Hurts like a bloomin' red hot knife's in there. Won't lose me arm, will I?"

Mark smiled. "No chance." He took the swab Asima handed him and washed away the dried blood from the wound. "Looks infected, though. You were right to bring him here. Problem is, I'm low on antibiotics. They're two days late with my supplies."

"I can send Harry to the hospital in Al Fashir. Get what you want."

"What I want?" Mark laughed dryly. "They don't even send me what I need — *desperately* need."

The tall soldier grasped Mark's arm in his big hand. "Just tell us what you need. Harry'll get it for you."

Mark met the sergeant major's steady gaze, and despite the tenseness of the situation around them, found himself enthralled by the unusual beauty of the man's eyes, and the very real thrill of his hand on Mark's bare arm. *Get a grip*, he told himself. The Aussie would most likely beat the shit out of him if he thought Mark fancied him.

"Uh…Asima, give the officer the list of medical supplies we urgently need, please." He pulled his gaze away from Caruthers when Asima ran to get the list. His face flushed hot as he bent to inspect O'Brien's wound again. "I need to get this bullet out quickly. I can use the antibiotics I have after the surgery, but you'll need at least a week's course to clear up the infection completely." He glanced at the sergeant major. "Can you get enough to make sure he stays clear of infection?"

"Sure, Doc… Harry will be there and back in a couple of hours." He watched as Asima injected O'Brien with a local anaesthetic. "Need a hand here? I've had some experience in field hospitals."

Mark smiled. "You're on. Let's go scrub up."

"Name's Jack, by the way. Or Boomer, if you like."

I like either one… Mark glanced at the handsome man standing by his side as he washed his hands, and he couldn't restrain the shiver of desire that coursed through him at the man's nearness. Keeping his voice steady he said, "Mark…but I don't mind you calling me 'Doc'."

"What's a bloke like you doing in a hellhole like this anyway?"

Mark chuckled. "A *bloke* like me?"

"You know — with your looks you'd be more at home in some fancy hospital in the US — Hollywood or somewhere like that."

"Ah, looks can be deceiving Serg — uh, Jack."

Jack's blue eyes twinkled with amusement. "This some kind of punishment?"

"You could say that. Self-inflicted, but that's another story, and one we don't have time for right now."

"I'd like to hear it sometime." Jack touched his arm gently as Mark moved out of the way to let him wash his hands.

Mark smiled and slipped on a pair of latex gloves. "The patient awaits."

"Be right there."

Mark left him as he talked into his radio informing someone on the other end of his location and O'Brien's condition.

Asima had O'Brien prepped and ready for Mark when he got back to the table. "How do you feel?" he asked the young Aussie as he slipped on a pair of latex gloves.

"Not bad. Pain's gone, probably 'cause I have this pretty nurse to ogle. Hope she's not a mind reader."

Asima giggled and blushed under her dark skin. Mark chuckled. "No, but she does speak English. Okay, hold steady now. You've had a local, but you might feel some discomfort when I start looking for the bullet."

O'Brien sucked in a breath as Mark began gently probing at the open wound. Jack joined them and stood silently by, watching every move Mark made.

"Yessss," Mark hissed. "Here it is. Bugger's in deep. This is going to hurt, soldier," he muttered, positioning the forceps around the base of the bullet. He looked up at Jack who nodded and held O'Brien steady within the grasp of his strong hands. The young soldier's eyes squeezed shut and he grimaced but didn't cry out as Mark slowly pulled the bullet from deep inside his flesh. Fresh blood seeped from the wound.

"That's good, isn't it, Doc?" Jack asked, peering at the wound.

Mark nodded. "Yes, helps clear the infection. I won't close up all the way. We'll put in a small drainage tube, keep it there for a couple of days. He should see a doctor when you get him back to base. Where is that exactly?"

"Here and there," Jack answered evasively.

"Too many ears?" Mark remarked, taking the suture needle from Asima.

"Right." He kept his eyes on Mark's hands as he skilfully sewed the wound closed, all but for a small space into which he carefully inserted a short drainage tube. "You do good work, Doc," he added as Mark stepped aside so Asima could bandage O'Brien's shoulder. He patted O'Brien on the head. "There y' go, Paddy, mate. You'll be up and at 'em in no time."

"Just take it easy, O'Brien," Mark said. "Asima will look after you."

"Yeah, thanks, Doc," O'Brien croaked. "Hope I can do the same for you some time."

As Asima attended to O'Brien, the two men walked the length of the clinic. When they reached Ghali's bed, the boy stared at them both, the wariness back in his eyes.

"Not bad man." Mark smiled at the boy. "Peace keeper."

Jack, his hand on Mark's shoulder, smiled down at Ghali, then knelt by Ghali's side. "What's all this about bad men?"

Ghali's expression dulled. "They come for me."

"Why? Why do they come for you?"

"They sell me. I run away, but they will find me."

Mark drew in a startled breath. He'd been trying to find out what was wrong with the boy for two days, and Jack had got the answer in less than two minutes. So much for his child psychology studies!

"Well, we'll take care of them baddies should they be stupid enough to show up," Jack was telling Ghali. "Don't you worry." He stroked the boy's hair briefly, then stood and indicated he and Mark should leave the boy's bedside.

"Fuckin' slave traders," Jack snarled when they were outside the clinic. "I'd like to skin every last one of 'em alive. *Bastards*."

"Poor kid," Mark murmured. "No wonder he's so scared and untrusting."

"Worst thing is," Jack said, kicking at the sand under his feet, "it was most likely his parents who gave him away."

The protest that sprang to Mark's lips died quickly as he gazed at the other man's stony expression. Yes, he was probably right. Abject poverty could make people act in terrible ways—ways they would never consider under normal circumstances. But there were no 'normal' circumstances in this part of the world where innocent men, women and children could be dragged from their homes and brutally murdered, where children were sold to buy a day or two's grain to make bread, and where a government turned a blind eye, or actively encouraged wholesale slaughter of its own people.

"Like a drink?" It was getting dark. Soon the nurses would be preparing the patients for yet another night of uneasy rest inside the clinic. He'd have to make sure Asima gave Ghali that sleeping pill…

"Thought you'd never ask." Jack's teeth gleamed white and even in the gathering dusk. His smile was slight, but warm, and his eyes held Mark's for a long moment, before he added, "What you got then?"

"Scotch."

"Let's go, my man. Your place or mine?"

Chuckling, they headed for Mark's tent, and a much needed drink.

Chapter Two

"Nice place you got here." Jack's lips twisted wryly as he looked around the small tent. Because of his height, he was forced to duck his head to avoid bumping it on the canvas roof.

"Have a seat." Mark indicated one of the two camp stools. "It'll be more comfortable." The stools, along with a narrow bed, a box full of books, a radio, and a rack from which hung Mark's clothes, was all the tent could hold.

"How long you been living like this?" Jack asked, watching Mark pour them both a drink into plastic cups.

"Three months and two days." Mark handed the Aussie one of the plastic cups filled with Scotch, and sat down on the other stool. "They keep telling me it's temporary, but so far I haven't seen any sign of the promised permanent hospital. I know this is only a refugee camp clinic, but half the time, I feel like I'm the forgotten man. Cheers." He touched his cup to

Jack's and smiled. "I'm glad you're here — I mean, I'm sorry for the reasons, but it's kinda nice to have good company."

"Cheers, mate." Jack threw the Scotch back in one long swallow, then grinned at Mark. "Good stuff." His piercing blue-eyed gaze swept over Mark, taking in the fine-boned, almost delicate planes of the young doctor's face, the shock of blond hair that fell disarmingly over his forehead, and the striking green of his eyes.

What a corker this bloke is, he thought. *A beautiful man, maybe too beautiful for his own good around these parts.* His cock swelled inside his shorts as his gaze fell on Mark's lush lower lip. *I'm going to taste that mouth before I leave this tent…*

"Like another?" Mark asked.

"Uh…yeah. Good on you." He watched, his lips parting in a silent gasp of lust as Mark bent to pick up the Scotch bottle, his shorts tightening across the curved swell of his butt. *That is one beautiful bum…*

"So, why do the men call you Boomer?" Mark refilled Jack's cup.

"Uh…oh, well, it's a bit of long story…"

"I've got time." He glanced at his watch. "Just have to check in with Asima before lights-out." He smiled. "I know, you're an explosives expert."

"Not exactly." Jack gulped his Scotch.

"Well, what exactly? There must be a reason for a nickname like Boomer."

"Well…uh…it's m' feet, if you must know."

"Your *feet?*" Mark chuckled as the sergeant's handsome face slowly filled with colour.

"Yeah, well…" He stretched out his long sun-darkened legs and both men looked down at the feet in question. "Boomer's the name we give kangaroos. They've got big feet and, well, mine...they're *big*, y'see..."

"Yeah," Mark murmured, "they sure are." *And not the only things*, he thought, his gaze travelling back up Jack's legs to the bulge in his shorts. He reached for the Scotch bottle and refilled the sergeant's empty cup.

Jack gave him a lopsided grin. "You trying to get me drunk?"

"Do I have to?"

Jack grabbed the front of Mark's shirt, pulling him in close until their mouths were a fraction apart, then he said, "No," and planted a forceful kiss on Mark's lips.

Startled, Mark gasped into Jack's mouth, but as the heat of the other man's lips seared his, Mark opened to him. Every nerve ending in Mark's body responded to the sensuous sensation of the other man's tongue as it swept inside Mark's mouth, finding and caressing each and every part of his moist warmth. He wound an arm around Jack's neck and held him, returning his kiss with a fierceness that surprised himself, his free hand sliding under Jack's shirt, stroking his muscled torso, bringing soft moans of pleasure from both men.

Mark pulled back slightly and smiled into Jack's blue eyes. "I think I've found another reason for your nickname."

"Oh yeah?" Jack's breath warmed Mark's lips. "What's that?"

Mark chuckled softly. "You make my heart go *boom*, Boomer."

"Smart one, ain't ya?" He toppled Mark over onto the floor and lay on top of him, grinding his bulging crotch into Mark's. "What else?"

Mark stared up at the bigger man with lust and longing. "I think you could ream my ass any time you want."

"You got that right," Jack growled, leaning down to take Mark's mouth again in a long brutal kiss that had them both gasping with desire. He tore open the front of Mark's shirt and started nuzzling his nipples. Mark groaned and held the sergeant's head to his chest, arching his body upwards.

They were so caught up with their own need the sound of the helicopter rotors outside the tent didn't immediately alert them to Harry's return.

"Shit," Jack muttered, jumping to his feet. He gave his hand to Mark, pulling him upright. Smiling ruefully, they straightened their clothes, Mark trying to get rid of his erection by brushing the front of his pants. "Later..." Jack hurried from the tent.

Mark stood there for a few moments allowing his breathing to return to normal and his hard-on to subside. *Holy shit*, he thought, *the guy is dynamite*. There would most definitely be a 'later'! He ran from the tent and watched Harry jump from the 'copter then hand a large package to Jack. The two men walked to where Mark waited.

"Here's your supplies, Doc," Harry told him.

"Thanks a million," Mark said fervently. "This'll make a huge difference." His eyes met Jack's over the top of the package. Jack gave him a salacious wink and a grin.

"How's O'Brien?" Harry asked.

"He'll be fine, better now we have more antibiotics," Mark replied. "I better go check on him and the others before lights-out." He looked towards the refugee camp where scores of small cooking fires flickered in the semi-darkness. Harry followed his gaze and shook his head.

"Poor bastards," he muttered. "When d'you suppose all this will end?"

"Never, if the government doesn't get its finger out of its bum." Jack's expression was grim. "And they're too fuckin' corrupt to do that. Most of the aid sent never gets to the people who need it. Those buggers in Khartoum are laughing up their sleeves, while the UN shells out money and sends idiots like us to 'keep the peace'."

"You are depressing the hell out of me, Sergeant Major." Mark started towards the clinic. "Maybe another drink will do the trick."

"Am I invited?" Harry asked.

"Of course," Mark said over his shoulder, then added tartly, "We'll need someone to liven up the evening." He chuckled to himself as he heard what sounded like a low growl escape Jack's throat. "See you *later*."

O'Brien was asleep when Mark checked in on him, as was Ghali. *Good*, he thought, looking down at the boy, whose long lashes dusted his fine cheekbones. An involuntary shudder passed over him as he considered what might have been Ghali's fate if he hadn't escaped from the slave traders. But just what was in his future? What promise of a good life could there be for a displaced child in a land like this, where every day more people sought refuge from rebels, and more families were torn apart by poverty and war?

He remembered his own childhood and how different it was from what children endured here in Darfur, and indeed in so many other countries where brutality and famine went hand in hand.

Never in his young life had he imagined there were places like this. Raised by a wealthy doting family, sent to the best schools, treated to vacations in luxurious resorts, Mark had grown up with a one-dimensional view of the world he lived in. Sure, he'd heard of the millions who were starving in the Middle East, but all of that seemed so far away, and besides, his father donated handsomely to the various charities serving the needy. What more could he possibly do, even if he'd wanted to? And back then, he hadn't wanted to...

"Where are you?" The big hand on the back of his neck and the gruff voice coming from behind startled him for a moment, then he leant back into the warmth and strength of Jack's touch.

"Right here, Jack," he replied, his voice a little unsteady. "Just thinking."

"About the kid, right?" Jack kept his voice low, aware of the sleeping patients, and the one or two nurses moving silently among them. He gave Mark's nape a gentle squeeze before taking his hand away. "About what the hell kind of life the little blighter's going to have, stuck in this god-forsaken piss hole."

"Something like that." He met Jack's eyes briefly. "Where's Harry?"

"Waitin' for that drink you promised him." He dropped his voice even lower. "What about you and me?"

Mark grinned. "We'll get Harry drunk, then we'll see."

"Huh. I'll tell him to kip down in the chopper. He's used to worse places."

"He can bunk down here in the clinic if he likes. There are no beds, but we can offer him some blankets and a pillow."

"Sounds like the life of Riley," Jack remarked, chuckling. "Come on then. Let's find him. Hope you have plenty Scotch. That bloke can knock 'em back."

Harry, cooling his heels outside the clinic, fell into step with them as they headed for Mark's tent. Mark ushered him inside.

"Sorry about the primitive conditions."

"They're not spoiling you, are they?" Harry remarked, looking around at the spartan space. He wasn't as tall as Jack, so could stand up without having to duck his head, but the sergeant immediately sat on the camp stool. To Harry's obvious surprise, Jack refused the drink Mark offered him.

"What's up, Sarge?" he asked, after swallowing his drink in one go. "Not like you to refuse a booze-up."

"Already had a couple, waiting for you. Gotta stay alert, I don't want to get plonked tonight."

"Don't mind if I do though?"

"Go right ahead. But we can't keep the doc up late. He's got patients to tend to in the morning, y'know."

Mark turned away to hide the smile Jack's words had caused. There was only one man allowed to keep 'the doc' up it seemed. Cool... He poured himself a short one. No way was he going to get 'plonked' either. He wanted to remember everything that happened tonight. Just the memory of the tall Australian's powerful body lying over him less than an hour ago had him hard inside his briefs. He sat down quickly.

Harry was full of news about what was going on in Al Fashir, and none of it was good. A bomb had exploded in a marketplace, killing and injuring dozens of women and children. The already overcrowded hospital was unable to cope with this latest disaster.

"It's lucky we know some of the staff there," Harry told them, "or there would have been no shot at getting medical supplies. Cost me every penny I had."

"Oh, I'll take care of that," Mark said. "I'll get you a reimbursement."

"Nah, no worries," Harry assured him. "Sarge here will take care of it, won't you, Sarge?" Jack nodded, and Harry stretched, yawning widely. "Shit, more tired than I thought. Think I'm ready for a kip." He held out his cup. "One for the road?" Mark grabbed the Scotch bottle and filled the proffered cup. Harry threw the Scotch back in one gulp.

"I'll show you where you can kip." Jack stood and almost hustled Harry from the tent.

"Oh, right... G'night, Doc. Thanks for the booze."

"'Night, Harry." Mark give a slight nod as Jack looked back at him, one eyebrow raised, before disappearing through the tent flap. He opened his medical bag and found a condom and some lube. He sniffed at his armpits, *shower – it's been a long day.* Quickly, he stripped off his shirt, boots and pants, wrapped a towel round his hips, then headed for the outside shower a few yards from his tent. This was a convenience he had insisted on when he'd arrived at the refugee camp clinic. Conditions were primitive enough, but there was no way he could exist without showering. He'd told the so-called authorities just that, and after much grumbling and scowling they had agreed to install a shower for his personal use. Mark encouraged the nurses and some of the patients who could get about to use it too.

Cold water only…of course, and it wasn't always there. Sighing with relief when the trickle of water squirted out of the nozzle over his head, he soaped himself quickly, paying close attention to his crotch and ass. He almost jumped out of his skin when two strong arms encircled his body, while something hot and hard pressed against his butt.

"Jesus, *Boomer!*" Mark stuttered out a surprised laugh. "You scared the shit outta me."

A big hand grasped his cock. "Not enough to make this big fella go away though." Jack's voice was husky as he nibbled at Mark's ear, slowly pumping Mark's growing erection. "Has anyone ever told you, you have the bum of an angel?"

Mark laughed. "Not quite in those words…" He groaned and let his head fall back against Jack's shoulder as the big sergeant continued to massage his cock. "Jack, there's really not enough room in here for what you've got in mind. Let's get back to my tent."

"Shower's a good idea, first." He turned Mark around and kissed him hard, holding both their erections in his hand and massaging them together, sending shockwaves through Mark's blood.

"*Boomer,*" he protested weakly.

"Okay, I can wait, just. Borrow the soap?"

"Here, let me…" Mark ran the soap over Jack's chest, smoothing the lather through the dusting of black hair and over his hardening nipples. "Lift your arms…" He worked the soap into Jack's armpits as the sergeant obliged.

Jack chuckled. "I'll smell like a lily after this."

Mark kissed his lips lightly. "Somehow I doubt that, Boomer. Here, stand under the water and rinse off. It'll run out in a minute." They shifted position, and

Mark wrapped his arms around the taller man's frame, sliding one hand down to grip the base of the thick uncut cock that rose proudly from Jack's dark pubic hair. He ran his lips over the broad back he was pressed against, his erection nestled in the cleft between Jack's muscular butt cheeks.

"Feels like you're good and ready for me." Jack's voice was husky with desire.

"I am. Let's get out of here." Mark turned off the water and stepped out of the shower. He picked up his towel. "Turn around," he said as Jack joined him. "I'll dry your back." The night air was still warm, and after a few swipes of the towel they were both soon dry. "Better get back," Mark murmured.

Jack picked up his clothes from where he'd dropped them and pulled on his shorts. "Let's go then." He put an arm around Mark's waist as they hurried through the darkness back to the tent.

Chapter Three

They wasted no time once they got back. Mark's towel and Jack's shorts were gone in an instant, and their eager bodies were pressed together in an embrace that had Mark's heart hammering in his chest with anticipation and excitement. It seemed to him as though Jack's mouth was everywhere at once, scorching his lips, his jaw, his throat, his nipples.

God! Mark's body arched against Jack's. A rush of adrenaline flooded his blood. Freeing himself from the taller man's crushing embrace, he dropped to his knees, desperate to claim Jack's cock, to hold it in his hands and his mouth, to take every inch of its prodigious length, to own it, if only for this one night. For even as he feverishly licked the swollen head, and savoured the salty cream glistening at the slit, he couldn't dispel the thought that this was totally crazy. Him and this soldier — this incredibly gorgeous man who would be gone in the morning, most probably forever. But, what the hell. He hadn't had sex in months, couldn't remember the last time he'd ever wanted it this much, and if this was to be the only time, then he'd relish it, enjoy every moment, take everything the man could give...

Jack spread his legs, bucking his hips forward, and Mark held on to the muscular thighs on either side of him as Jack pushed his pulsing cock between Mark's lips, the head sliding over Mark's tongue, nudging at his soft palate. Mark closed his lips around the hot flesh, sucking hard, gliding back and forth, his tongue laving the underside of Jack's steel-like shaft, his hands caressing Jack's thighs, then reaching behind to cup the firm, round globes of his ass. He pulled back almost to the cockhead, then with one long downward glide took all of it to the root, burying his nose in the muskiness of Jack's pubic hair. A long low groan escaped Jack, before he hoisted a protesting Mark to his feet.

"You'll have me comin' all over the place." The Aussie's voice was a tad unsteady as he trapped Mark in his arms.

"That was the idea," Mark murmured, hungrily kissing Jack's mouth, pressing his erection fiercely against Jack's.

"Not so quick, though," Jack said when they broke off the kiss. "I want this to last, to remember it..."

Touched by the man's sentiment, Mark slowed a little, tilting his head back and gazing into the bluest of blue eyes. "Yes," he whispered, "I want to remember this too." And not for just a day or two after Jack had left, but for a long time to come.

Their next kiss was still laced with hunger, but sweeter, more measured, taking time to taste each other's mouths, their tongues dancing lightly together, while they held one another, searching hands sliding over smooth skin and hard muscle.

"Wait." Mark stepped over to his cot, dragging the mattress off and laying it on the ground. He dropped down on it and, smiling up at the big sergeant, opened his arms. Jack was on him in an instant, both men groaning their pleasure as hot, bare flesh and moist mouths meshed and bonded.

Jack laved Mark's neck and chest with his lips and tongue, scouring each tiny nipple, nibbling on them gently, causing Mark to writhe under him and make little whimpering noises in the back of his throat. He kissed his way south over Mark's supple torso, dipping his tongue into the small indented navel, lingering there before a muffled entreaty had him following the treasure trail of blond hair leading to Mark's hard cock. With one wide swipe of his tongue he scooped up the pre cum from the glistening head, then inch by inch his lips slid down the silken length of Mark's erection.

"Jesus..." Mark gasped, his fingers digging into Jack's shoulder. Jack fondled Mark's balls while he sucked, letting his middle finger caress Mark's perineum then probe the cleft between his ass cheeks. Mark bucked at the sensation, his hand moving to Jack's head, fingers raking the sergeant's close-cropped curly hair. Jack shifted position to kneel in front of Mark. He lifted the smaller man's legs over his shoulders, leaning in to take his balls one by one into his mouth, rolling them gently between his lips. Mark moaned, his hands clutching at the sides of the mattress, then reaching out grasping at air as Jack's tongue moved to Mark's opening, bathing the puckered hole with his saliva.

"Boomer, *Jack*...oh, Jesus..." Mark's head thrashed from side to side as if in delirium. His hands found Jack's and held them in a crushing grip. "Fuck me...oh yeah, I need you inside me now...need that beautiful cock..."

Jack raised his head, his eyes locking on Mark's glazed expression. Silently, he took the lube Mark handed him, squeezed some onto his fingers, then eased his way inside Mark's tight opening, one finger, then two, carefully stretching him in readiness, smiling as Mark wriggled his ass, drawing Jack's fingers deeper inside him.

The condom was a tight fit, and Jack applied more lube before settling between Mark's thighs, then guiding himself towards the young man's eager hole. He paused when Mark's body stiffened under him. "Okay?"

"Yes, yes..." Beads of sweat formed on Mark's brow and he bit his lower lip, but managed a smile. "It hurts, but it'll get better, I know."

Jack didn't want to hurt Mark, so he waited a few moments, letting Mark get used to the thickness pressing into him. When he felt him relax a little he pushed forward and Mark arched his body upwards to meet his slow downward plunge.

"Oh yeah..." Mark smiled at him, the tip of his tongue snaking out to lick his lower lip. "Mmm...feels good." He reached up and wound his arms around Jack's neck, pulling him down for a long, loaded kiss, the effect giving impetus to the rocking rhythm Jack had begun. As their lips and tongues meshed, as each long thrust quickened in tempo, they moaned their mounting lust and desire into each other's mouths.

Jack knew at that moment he had never enjoyed sex as much with anyone else in his life. The sensations of holding this lithe, virile young man in his arms, the sweet passion of his kisses, the taste and scent of him filled his senses and started to carry him over the edge. He could tell by the way Mark gasped into his mouth, his chest heaving with exertion, he was close to coming.

And yes, he exulted, reaching for and gripping Mark's pulsing erection, *this is how it should be*. Crazily, the words of the old Beatles song 'Come Together' spun into his mind, and he choked out a triumphant laugh. Mark joined in, and a moment later they were riding the crests of their mutual orgasms, crying out with delirious joy as Mark's semen coated both their torsos, and Jack emptied himself into the condom buried deep inside his lover.

"Holy shit." Sweat-drenched and exhausted, Mark shifted slightly in Jack's arms to prolong the sweet feeling of having the big man still hard, and still deep inside him. He kissed Jack's nose and smiled. "You rocked my world there, buddy. Fucked me royally. I'm going to be walking funny for a couple of days." Jack smoothed back the damp blond curls

from Mark's forehead, then kissed his lips gently. Mark gazed into his blue eyes. "Was it good for you too?"

"Better than good..." Jack's breath was warm on Mark's lips. "Didn't hurt you, did I?"

Mark smiled. So his big, butch Aussie had a sensitive side. Nice. "Not really," he replied, tightening his ass muscles around Jack's cock. "But it might the second time around."

They must have dozed off, for when Jack stirred, Mark was pressed to his side, his head on Jack's chest, the breath from his slightly parted lips warming Jack's left nipple. The sergeant stared up at the canvas roof above him, and felt an unfamiliar ache as he thought about what this morning would bring. He would have to leave — get back to base, have O'Brien hospitalised, wait for further orders — and leave this beautiful man behind.

He sighed as Mark muttered in his sleep and tightened an arm around Jack's broad chest. This felt so damned good, and was something he'd been without for longer than he could remember. Yes, there had been a quick fuck here and there when he'd been on leave, but that had been more than a year ago, and had been barely memorable at the time. What he felt this time was different — but whatever it was, he'd have to get over it. There was no way he could have any kind of relationship right now. Not stuck in this god-forsaken part of the world. He had his responsibilities, and the man he held in his arms certainly had his.

What the hell had persuaded Mark to ever volunteer for this? *Doctors Who Care International*, like *Doctors Without Borders*, was known and admired for the dedication of its medical staff, but he'd never seen a doctor left to cope with so little help and meagre supplies. Maybe he could persuade Mark to request a transfer to a place where there were improved medical facilities, although he had a feeling it wouldn't be easy. As rough as things were here, Mark seemed resigned to wait until the permanent hospital was built and his patients properly looked after.

So where did that leave them? Both working for the same cause really, but separated by impossible distances of desert and wilderness. This refugee camp wasn't even on their patrol…

"Hey…" Mark's softly murmured greeting interrupted Jack's troubled thoughts.

"Hey, yourself." He kissed Mark's forehead and stretched. "Thought you'd never wake up," he teased.

Mark pushed himself deeper into Jack's warmth. "I haven't slept this well in weeks. Where have you been all my life?"

"Too far away, obviously."

"And you have to leave this morning…"

"'Fraid so."

"I guess it would be stupid of me to suppose we could meet somewhere, sometime?"

"Not stupid, Doc. I was lying here wondering how we could do just that."

Mark licked Jack's left nipple. "Did you come up with anything?"

"You asking for a transfer to—"

"Can't do that, Jack." Mark's response was immediate, cutting him off. "I promised Asima and the other nurses I'd stay 'til I'd badgered the fuck-heads in charge enough that they finally build a hospital here for these people. I can't leave until it's done."

"Right. I figured that would be your answer." He ran his forefinger over Mark's lower lip. "We'll just have to think of something else then." He sat up, looking around for his clothes, then glanced at his watch. "I'd better get a move on."

Mark reached up to caress Jack's muscular back, trailing his fingers sensuously down Jack's spine. "Must you?"

Jack sighed. He got to his feet, aware of Mark's eyes on his naked body. "Yeah, gotta get Paddy and Harry back to base." He slipped on his shorts, then held out a hand to Mark and pulled him to his feet. They stood locked in each other's arms for a long moment, before Jack said gruffly, "Tonight's going to be a real let down."

"Know what you mean," Mark whispered.

Their kiss was hard and hungry, for both men knew this was all they would have for now — and the foreseeable future.

* * * *

Asima had O'Brien's dressing changed when Mark checked in. "Not much drainage," she told him. "Infection not bad."

The young Australian gave Asima a fond look. "Swell sheilas you have here, Doc. Looked after me good and proper."

And your sergeant major looked after me good and proper, Mark thought, smiling at the private, then asked Asima, "How did Ghali sleep last night?"

"Very good," Asima assured him. "No crying out at all."

"Terrific, thanks, Asima..." He took a quick stroll between the beds, checking on the patients. Some were still asleep, some gave him small smiles. Ghali was awake, his big dark eyes appraising Mark as he approached.

"Asima tells me you had a good night, Ghali."

"Everyone here is in danger," Ghali said, quietly.

"You mean from the slave-traders? We have a security force here, Ghali. There is no danger."

Ghali gazed sadly at Mark. "When they come, you must hide too."

Startled, Mark asked, "Why do you say that? If they come, they will be arrested. Don't worry, Ghali, everything will be all right."

"Slave traders will want you. You are pretty man."

Mark chuckled. "Pretty? Girls are pretty, Ghali. Not men." He turned as he heard Jack call him. "I'll be back. Try not to worry about the bad men." He walked over to where Jack stood with Harry and Patrick.

"Time to go, Doc." Jack held out his hand. "Thanks for looking after Paddy for us," he added, squeezing Mark's hand gently. "We'll make sure you get your supplies on time."

"Thanks," Mark muttered, wanting to throw himself into Jack's arms, but instead shaking his hand politely, then acknowledging the other men's thanks. They walked outside the clinic and Harry ran to get the 'copter's engines warmed up. "Take it easy, O'Brien. Make sure you get that wound looked at soon as you get back to base." *Wherever that is*, he thought wryly. *I won't even know where he is, god dammit...* He and Jack exchanged one last look of longing and regret, then Mark watched as the two soldiers walked towards the helicopter, depression settling on him like a black cloud. He was barely aware that a man from the refugee camp was running swiftly towards him, agitation clearly etched on his dark features.

"*Effendi, effendi*," the man panted, tugging at Mark's arm. He pointed in the direction of the camp. "Men come, looking for boy. They say they know he is here.

They will come to the clinic looking for him when they cannot find him among us."

Mark stiffened with shock. The slave traders here? "Thank you," he muttered. "I'll alert our security patrol."

"Put boy on helicopter," the man urged Mark. "Security no good..."

Mark was inclined to agree with that, but his instructions had been to always alert the security patrol in the event of trouble. Dhul Fiqar, the patrol leader, was an arrogant jerk, but he did have several men with guns at his disposal. Still, if Jack could take Ghali to safety, it might prevent the slave traders rampaging through the clinic terrifying the patients.

"Jack!" he yelled, waving frantically at the sergeant who was helping O'Brien onto the helicopter. "Wait up!" For a moment he thought Jack hadn't heard him over the noise of the chopper's engine, then he turned and started jogging back, while Mark ran to meet him.

"What's up?" Jack demanded, catching Mark by the arm.

"The slave traders," Mark gasped. "They're in the refugee camp. It's only a matter of time before they come here. Can you take Ghali with you? If they come up empty handed, they'll start looking elsewhere..."

"Bastards... Yeah, go get the kid, we'll take him."

Mark started back to the clinic. He pulled the two-way radio he carried from his belt as he ran. "Fiqar? Come in, please, it's Doctor Hamilton. We have an emergency."

"What is it?" Fiqar's voice squawked back at him.

"Slave traders in the refugee camp. They're looking for one of my patients. I'm having him flown to safety, but I need you and your men here to stop these criminals from busting up the place."

"There is no need for concern, Doctor." Even through the bad reception Mark could hear the sneer in Fiqar's voice. "We will take care of the situation. Leave the boy where he is."

No way, Mark thought. He had no faith whatsoever in Fiqar's military expertise. Ghali would be much safer with Jack and his men. And what was it about Dhul Fiqar that made Mark immediately suspect the man of an ulterior motive in telling him to have Ghali remain in the clinic?

"Too late," he lied. "The peace keeping team already has the boy. They're taking him even as we speak."

"Doctor Hamilton, you are disobeying my orders!"

"I'm not under your jurisdiction, Fiqar," Mark snapped back. "The safety of my patients is all I care about." He broke the connection. "Jack, take Ghali now before that jerk gets here. He'll only make things worse."

"C'mon, kid." Jack lifted Ghali from the bed. "You and me are goin' to take a chopper ride. Like that?"

Ghali nodded, wrapping his arms around Jack's neck. "Doctor come too," he whispered in Jack's ear. "Bad men will take him."

Jack stared at Mark. "The kid's worried about you. So am I for that matter. I don't think we'll leave 'til those slavers are gone from here."

"No, Jack. If they see Ghali here —"

"I'll put him in the chopper with Harry. He'll be safe there."

Mark was beginning to get a very bad feeling about how this was going to turn out. "How many of the patients can you take?" he asked.

Jack frowned, hearing the tension in Mark's voice. "About six or seven. Why?"

"Jack, do this for me, will you? I want you to take some of the more badly injured with you. Asima too — she can look after them 'til you get them to a hospital."

"And you," Jack said tersely.

"I can't leave, Jack. The other patients need a doctor. I can't desert them now. Just go, take Ghali and the others, I'll be okay. Fiqar, the security patrol leader, will be here in a few minutes..."

"So why all the precautions?" Jack asked.

Mark sighed. "Because I don't trust Fiqar to protect the patients. He's way too scared of getting his uniform dirty..."

"Okay." Jack stared at Mark, his jaw set in a 'don't fucking argue with me' hard line. "Here's what we're gonna do. We'll get your patients and the nurses on board the chopper, but we're not leaving 'til I'm certain the situation is under control. If this Fucker, or whatever his name is, can't handle the slavers, we're takin' off — with you on board. Got that?"

"But..."

"Don't argue with me, Doc. That's the way it's gonna be, even if I have to put you over my shoulder and carry you to the chopper myself."

Despite himself, Mark grinned. "Yes sir!" He saluted Jack smartly. "Now go take Ghali to the helicopter, while Asima and I get the others ready."

Jack grinned back at him. "Just don't take all day."

Asima, who had been listening to the men's conversation, had already arranged with Fatima, the other nurse on duty, to have the more badly injured patients ready to leave.

"The others want to go back to the camp, Doctor," she informed Mark.

Mark nodded. "Probably a good idea. Their families can look after them until this is over. With any luck Fiqar might stop the slavers getting this far, but we can't be too careful." What he stopped short of saying was, 'And we can't trust that jerk further than we can throw him.'

"You must come too, Doctor." Asima laid a gentle hand on his arm.

"I guess I can now that there are no patients left to worry about. I'll just go get my medical bag. Hurry now, and get to the helicopter."

Chapter Four

Back in his tent, Mark hastily threw some medical supplies into his bag. No way to know what he might need on the flight to Al Fashir. The sound of approaching vehicles made him pull his gun from the bag and stow it under his belt. His stomach jolted with apprehension as he exited the tent and found himself surrounded by three vehicles, and if he wasn't mistaken, Dhul Fiqar's Jeep was among them.

What the hell...? Why had that moron brought the slavers here? He should have prevented them getting anywhere near the clinic. *I knew that s.o.b. couldn't be trusted*, he seethed. Or was he maligning the patrol leader — had they perhaps taken him prisoner? Either way, this wasn't good. He glanced at the helicopter, its rotors slowly gyrating, ready to take off. Maybe he should just make a run for it. He could see Jack and Harry loading the last of the patients on board, then Jack turned and signalled for Mark to join them.

"One moment, Doctor Hamilton." Dhul Fiqar's smooth as silk voice made Mark's hackles rise. "You have something these gentlemen require."

"They're too late," Mark snapped, glaring at Fiqar through narrowed eyes. "And what the hell are you doing with them? You're supposed to be protecting the people here—"

"Silence!" Mark's glare went from Fiqar to a burly man wearing fatigues who had stepped down from his vehicle. "You, American," the man growled, "where is the boy, Ghali?"

"Like I said, you're too late," Mark told him. "Ghali's on board that helicopter, protected by Australian peace keepers. I wouldn't try anything foolish if I were you. They're Special Ops, and—"

Snarling, the man struck Mark across his face. "Take him!" he ordered Fiqar.

Mark reached for his gun, but Fiqar and two other men grabbed him, the gun wrested from his hand. Mark struggled like a maniac, but he was forced to his knees, the barrel of a weapon he couldn't see pressed to the top of his skull.

"Tell those soldiers from *Special Ops*," the big man sneered, "to hand over the boy, or I shall pull this trigger and you will no longer have any say in the matter whatsoever."

"Not on your life, scumbag," Mark hissed.

He winced as he heard the click of the trigger's release. *Oh, shit…*

From Jack's position at the 'copter, he could see Mark was in trouble. The vehicles that had pulled up at the clinic didn't look as though they belonged to any security patrol. They were way too heavily armed for one thing, and as he trained his binoculars on them he could see the men on board were not in any kind of uniform. His eyes widened as he saw Mark being forced to his knees.

"Fuckin' slavers," he muttered. "Tell Harry to take off on my say so," he yelled at Paddy. "Looks like the Doc's got more than he can handle."

"Sarge…" Paddy gave him a worried look.

"Just tell him," Jack snapped, setting off at a run towards where Mark was being held by the slave traders. *No way were they going to hurt him.*

Mark heard the sharp sound of a shot and one of the men holding him cried out, then crumpled to the ground. He used the sudden shock to kick himself free of the other man's grip. He rolled away as another shot rang out, and a yell of pain came from somewhere among the group of slavers.

"Shoot him down!" The burly man was screaming at the top of his voice, and as Mark sprang to his feet he could see it was Jack who was inciting the man's anger.

Mark launched himself at Fiqar, grabbing for the gun the creep had taken from him. Fiqar grunted with surprise as he went down, the gun falling from his grasp. Mark reached for it, but a blow to the side of his head momentarily stunned him, then Fiqar was on top of him, his hands around Mark's throat. Mark brought his knee up, ramming it into Fiqar's crotch. Fiqar squealed and fell away, clutching his balls, allowing Mark to grab his gun and get to his knees. He fired at the man who had struck him, but missed, the bullet smashing the windshield of one of the vehicles. Jack yelled at him to run and he leapt to his feet, sprinting towards where Jack was crouched, keeping up a steady fire at the slavers. Bullets whined and kicked up the sand around him as he ran, expecting any moment to feel the burning pain of impact on his body from one of the slavers' guns.

Gasping for breath he flung himself onto the sand alongside Jack. His heart sank upon hearing the click of an empty chamber from Jack's gun. "Here." He handed Jack his Browning. "You're a better shot than me." Jack squeezed off two more shots, and was rewarded by the sound of at least one cry of pain as his shot hit true.

"That's it," Jack grunted. "All out of ammo." He grabbed his radio as the slavers advanced on them, sure now they had Mark and Jack at their mercy. "*Harry*," he yelled. "Get the hell out of here. Get those people to safety – go! And don't forget to come back and get us!"

Mark turned to see the chopper rise into the air, banking sharply to make it less of a target as the slavers sent volley after volley at the quickly disappearing craft. He breathed a sigh of relief when the men stopped firing after a guttural command from their leader. Dhul Fiqar, still rubbing his crotch, shot Mark an evil look as the slavers surrounded them.

"You are going to be sorrier than you could ever imagine, Doctor Hamilton," he said, his voice dripping venom. "You will wonder why you saved that boy, now that you have to take his place!"

"What the hell are you talking about?"

"My friend, Hannad Malouf, a Turkish business man, has reckoned that your actions have cost him a great deal of money, therefore both of you will pay the price."

"Turkish businessman, my arse." Jack added a derisive snort. "He's a fuckin' slave trader – "

"Silence!" Fiqar pointed at Jack."You will be held for ransom. The United Nations will no doubt pay to have their brave soldier returned to them. But for you, Doctor Hamilton, Mr. Malouf has a very special treat in store. You will take the place of Ghali, and will be sold into slavery, to satisfy in every way, the carnal whims of the man who purchases you."

"Are you out of your fuckin' mind?" Jack railed at Malouf. "The doctor's an American citizen. You carry out this shit and you'll be on the run for the rest of your miserable life. And *you...*" He jabbed a finger at Fiqar. "When your bosses find out what you've done, you won't have a corner to hide in, you bloody arsehole. What the fuck are you thinkin', getting in league with scum like this—?"

A barked command from Malouf and one of the slavers stepped forward and struck Jack, hard, on the forehead with the butt of his gun. Jack staggered back then went down on his knees, hand raised to staunch the blood that dripped into his eyes.

"*Jack...*" Mark knelt by him, trying to see the damage. "Let me take care of his wound," Mark pleaded, looking up at the burly man.

"How touching," Malouf sneered, licking his thick lips as Jack slumped against Mark. "Take them to the clinic, but bind that one's hands," he added, gesturing at Jack.

* * * *

"You're going to need a couple of stitches," Mark told Jack after he'd examined his head. He glanced at the two armed men Malouf had sent to keep an eye on them. "I have to get a suture needle and some antiseptic." The men stared back at him. "Is that okay?" he asked impatiently.

"They don't speak English," Jack pointed out.

"Oh, right…" He mimed pulling a needle through Jack's head, and used what few words of Arabic he knew. "Okay?" he repeated. One of the men shrugged, and Mark took that to mean he could go ahead. He opened one of the cabinets and took out an already threaded needle and a bottle of antiseptic.

"This'll sting a bit," he muttered, gently swabbing Jack's forehead.

"Go for it…and listen to me without showing any reaction to what I'm saying." Jack gazed up into Mark's eyes. "I have to get you out of here before they separate us. What they've got in mind for you means you'll be taken for inspection to whoever they had Ghali lined up for. Unfortunately, I don't have a clue where that might be. We can't be separated—Ow!" He winced as Mark inserted the suture needle. "Easy, Doc…"

"Sorry."

"S'okay. Now listen…"

"Wait until I've finished. You keep jerking my hand with all that moving about. Hold still…" Mark steadied Jack's head with a hand cupping one cheek and leant in close. Jack's leg pushed between Mark's thighs, rubbing sensuously. "*Jack,*" Mark breathed, "not right now. You're making my hand shake. Besides, they'll see…"

"Fuck 'em."

"No thanks. Have you smelled them?"

Jack chuckled, then his expression turned serious. "Like I said, we can't be separated. I'm going to act like this is a lot worse than it is—pretend I'm concussed, fall over, that kind of thing. Hopefully, it'll make 'em lower their guard some, then I can take the buggers by surprise, get their guns, and we can hop outta here, tout bloody suite."

"You make it sound real easy, Boomer, my friend." Mark dabbed more antiseptic over the completed stitches. "But you have your hands tied behind your back, and somehow I don't think either of those two is going to be kind enough to cut the rope."

"No, you have to do that."

"Gladly, but how?"

They were interrupted by Malouf and Fiqar appearing in the doorway. Malouf uttered a few sharp commands Mark didn't understand, and the two guards grabbed Jack by each arm, hauling him off the table.

"You must bid your brave soldier friend farewell," Fiqar said.

"What do you mean?" Mark asked warily.

Malouf sighed with impatience. "What he means is that you are to be transported to a different destination." His smile was vicious. "One where you may find yourself staying for a long, long time."

"No, you bastards," Jack yelled. "You can't do this!"

"Be quiet," Malouf snapped. "Your opinion is of no significance. You will remain here, under guard, until either your ransom is paid, or the guards tire of you, and shoot you."

Mark gasped. "You guys act like this is still the Middle Ages. And if you think whoever wanted Ghali is going to settle for me, you're nuts. I'm a lot older than that kid, and—"

"You underestimate yourself, Doctor," Malouf interrupted smoothly. "You are a very beautiful young man." He ran a hand over Mark's hair and face, ignoring Mark's flinch of revulsion. "Blond hair, green eyes, golden skin—yes, my client will want you. Of that, I have no doubt."

Malouf jumped back, startled, when Jack kicked out at him, just missing the large man's belly. The guards, also momentarily taken by surprise, loosened their grip on Jack's arms. That was all he needed. Jack's military training proved that even with his hands tied behind his back, he was a lethal force. He lashed out with a well executed karate kick that caught one of the guards under the chin, knocking him senseless. The other raised his rifle, ready to club Jack, then screamed as another kick from Jack's big foot connected with his knee. Mark winced as he heard the guard's kneecap shatter under the blow.

Fiqar pulled out his gun, and the commotion brought Malouf's men running into the clinic. Fiqar held Mark at gunpoint while the extra men weighed in against Jack. It took four of them to force him to his knees and hold him down, and even then all had guns drawn on him, wary of Jack's speed and strength.

Malouf looked shaken by Jack's attack. Now he was down two more men. "Take him outside," he snarled. "This time, tie him so he can't move!" His vicious glare fixed on Mark, then on Fiqar. "Let's go. The sooner we can deliver him and get paid, the better."

While Jack was hustled out of the clinic, struggling like a maniac all the way, Fiqar led Mark outside to a waiting SUV.

Mark tried to see what they were doing with Jack, but Malouf pushed him inside the vehicle, getting in the back seat alongside him, a gun trained on Mark's chest. Fiqar and one of Malouf's men sat up front,

Fiqar in the driver's seat. Mark anxiously peered out the rear window, but he could see no sign of Jack.

Jesus, he thought frantically, *how has all this gone so terribly wrong?*

* * * *

Jack groaned, then gritted his teeth against the pain in his head as he regained consciousness. Malouf's men, after seeing what Jack had done to their compatriots, had knocked him out in order to tie him up — without getting kicked in the face by the crazy Australian. Practically his whole body was tied up with so much rope he could hardly breathe.

"Arseholes," he muttered, realising he was in the back of either a truck or a lorry that jarred every bone in his body as it bumped over rough terrain.

Damn the bastards. He could only hope Mark was in a vehicle somewhere up ahead. Malouf had obviously decided the odds would have been against him if he'd waited at the clinic. He'd most likely figured that once Harry got back to base camp the chopper pilot would alert his commanding officer to what had happened, and a special task force would be sent out to rescue their sergeant and the doctor.

The back of the truck was covered with a tarp and the heat was oppressive. Despite the fact he was wearing only a tanktop and shorts, he was sweating like a pig. *Only pigs don't sweat, do they?* he thought wryly, rubbing his aching wrists still tied behind his back. He drew in a surprised breath as he felt the rope slip over his sweaty skin.

Hmm... He tugged hard, his hand slid upwards, and the rope caught under his thumb. *Dammit...* He slid his hand back down and tried again. *Yes...one hand* was almost out; another tug and his hand slipped away from the rope. Feverishly, he worked at the ropes binding his other wrist. It took longer but he was finally able to free both hands. Now he jerked at the ropes binding his legs, pushing them down over his sweating skin until they reached his boots.

Now here was the real challenge. *How to get 'em over these bloody big feet!* Maybe if he could get his boots off... Grimacing as every attempt resulted in rope burn he managed to press the heel of his right boot against the heel of the left. He pushed, but the tightness of the ropes limited his movement. Swearing, he fell onto his back, and stared up at the tarp, realising he'd lost what little light there had been when he'd come to. They must have been on the road for some time.

Muttering to himself, he hooked his heels together again and pushed. He grinned when he felt his left boot budge. *Aha...*

* * * *

Mark looked out of the SUV's window at the darkening sky. *Where are you, Jack?* he wondered. *Did they leave you back there, or worse still, kill you?* He wouldn't put it past these cutthroats to have just disposed of Jack out of spite, after he'd whupped their asses. It had been bad enough thinking that because of their different careers they might not ever see one another again—but now, if Jack was still their prisoner, or dead... Mark decided he didn't want to think of that possibility. Jack was a survivor—a warrior. He'd never go down easily.

"How much longer?" he asked, almost unable to stand the acrid stench of stale sweat in the SUV's cab. He knew he probably didn't smell that fresh himself, but Malouf's driver was rank. Even Fiqar looked as though he was trying hard not to breathe too deeply. "We've been driving for hours."

"We are almost there," Malouf grunted. "What? Are you anxious to meet your owner?"

"No, I'm anxious to get out of this damned stinking SUV. And no one's going to *own* me, Malouf. We did away with slavery a long time ago."

Malouf smirked. "Perhaps in your country, but you are not in America now, young doctor. I'm afraid the man you are about to meet has very strong ideas of dealing with what is his."

"You're taking an awful lot for granted, aren't you? What if this man doesn't care for someone old enough to have been round the block a few times? I thought that kind of man only liked very young boys or girls. I'm twenty-seven, and I'm no virgin."

Malouf's chuckle was louder this time. "Oh, he will like you, of that I have no doubt. You may have been *round the block* as you put it, a few times, but you have the look of an innocent. Yes, he will like you… And if you are good to him, you will lack for nothing. Be sensible now and accept your fate. It will go easier for you if you do."

Mark turned away, biting his lip. It was pointless arguing with a moron like Malouf. The man had no morality, no humanity. To him, Mark was just another piece of merchandise. All he wanted was the money Mark could bring him.

Mark wondered if instead of arguing with Malouf he should try bartering. "My father is a very rich man. He would pay you for my release."

"Too much trouble," Malouf grunted. "I have already sealed the bargain. Now, enough talking. We are here…"

Mark's stomach churned as they passed through massive gates into torch-lit grounds that even in the darkness he could see were lushly landscaped. Where on earth were they that such opulence could exist in the middle of the wilderness? He could only guess they were somewhere near Khartoum, although he had seen no sign of city lights on the way. Mark's eyes widened when they pulled up at the portico of a huge house, its grandeur illuminated by more flaming torches.

Wow. Whoever lives here has to be as rich as Croesus. Mark suddenly realised his hands were balled up into tight fists. He unclenched them, rubbed his sweaty palms together, his mind filled with crazy thoughts that somehow Jack would appear out of nowhere, guns blazing, and get them both the hell out of there. Of course, that didn't happen, and Mark was hauled out of the SUV by Malouf and Fiqar, then bundled up the steps into the house. *House? More like a palace.*

Mark looked around at the marble walls and the immensely high domed ceiling he guessed was the entryway. They were obviously expected. Two young men dressed in white flowing shirts and pants approached, bowed, then gestured that Mark should follow them. He hesitated until he felt a prod from Malouf's gun barrel on his back.

"Don't waste time, Doctor," Malouf said through gritted teeth. "These men have been sent to prepare you."

Mark swung around and glared at the burly Turk. "Prepare me for what exactly?"

"Don't be naïve, Doctor Hamilton," Malouf sneered. "You know exactly why you are here. Now go with these men, before I have to force you at gunpoint."

One of the young men laid a gentle hand on Mark's arm and gestured again that he should follow them.

"Well, I guess I don't have much choice at this point," he muttered. *Oh, Jack, why aren't you swinging in here on the chandelier, ready to knock the shit outta Malouf and Figar?* Sighing, he followed the two men down a wide corridor, the floor of which was solid marble, and the walls lined with rich tapestries. *No expense spared here*, he thought, looking around as the men paused outside a door for a moment before opening it and ushering Mark in.

A bathroom—but what a bathroom. Mark whistled through his teeth as he took in the marbled magnificence surrounding him. *Man, if all this wasn't quite so creepy, I could get used to it!* He looked at his two young escorts. They were slim, good-looking dudes, and he could probably take them. There was no sign of a weapon on either of them. He tensed, ready to throw a punch at the nearest man, when from the corner of his eye he glimpsed a movement, then a tall figure, half hidden by one of the many marble pillars around the bathroom. There was no mistaking what the man had slung over his shoulder—an Uzi. *Damn.* He relaxed his aggressive stance, knowing that even if he could overpower the two attendants, he'd be cut down in seconds. Made sense, he thought. Why would they risk him being left unguarded when he was here under duress?

Smiling, and showing pearly white teeth, the young men bowed. One of them pointed to himself and said softly, "Omar."

The other repeated the gesture. "Hassan. We are brothers."

They started to undo Mark's shirt buttons. "Uh, I can do that..." But they acted as if they suddenly didn't speak English. Ignoring his protests, they slipped Mark's shirt over his shoulders, then started to unbuckle his belt. "Wait, wait...I'll do it." He didn't want to slap at the guys' hands, but they seemed to get the hint and allowed him to undo his belt and drop his shorts. Omar knelt at his feet and began pulling off Mark's boots. "Okay," he muttered. "You can do that..." He didn't fail to notice that the one kneeling at his feet was taking his time, his eyes level with Mark's crotch. *He wouldn't, would he?*

Hassan uttered something sharply to his brother who straightened up, then carried Mark's boots to where they'd left his clothes. Now on either side of him, they conducted Mark to the enormous bath in the centre of the room and indicated he should get in.

"Uh...some privacy, maybe?" His request went without comment from either brother. They simply stared at him and indicated again that he should get in the tub.

Mark sighed, but had to admit as he settled into the subtly scented water that it felt good — damned good. It had been a long time since he'd had a hot bath, and his only regret was that Jack wasn't here to share it with him. In another life, they could have had fun together in this big tub...

Still smiling, Omar and Hassan waited patiently while Mark bathed.

Chapter Five

Jack froze as he heard the sound of men approaching the truck. *Okay...a couple of options here,* he thought, tightening the ropes he'd loosened around him. One, he could jump them when they started to get him out of the truck, knock the shit out of 'em, grab their guns, then find out where they'd taken Mark. Problem was he wasn't a hundred percent certain Mark was anywhere near. They might have taken him somewhere else entirely... Okay, option two, he could beat the shit out of them, take their guns, then use a little gentle persuasion to find out where Mark was. *Yeah, I like that one better.*

He waited until the men pulled the tarp from over him and one of them gripped his ankles to pull him out of the truck. Jack let himself be pulled halfway out, then jack-knifed his body, kicking the startled guard squarely in the chest with both big feet. The man staggered back, almost doing a back flip from the impact. The other guard swung his rifle at Jack's head as he jumped from the bed of the truck. Jack pole axed him with a chop to the side of the slaver's neck. He went down like a wet sack and didn't get up. The first guard, wheezing mightily, charged at Jack, drawing a long-bladed knife as he did so. He crashed into Jack and the two of them went sprawling on the ground, the guard on top of Jack, the knife an inch from his throat.

The man yelped as Jack's fist connected with his jaw, causing him to slump to the side and roll away. Jack was on him in an instant, one hand round the slaver's throat, the other squeezing his wrist hard until with cry of pain the man released his hold on the knife hilt. Jack heard movement behind him. His head snapped round, the knife he now held arcing upward, plunging into the belly of the other guard who was poised, about to ram the butt of his rifle against Jack's head. Jack wrenched the knife blade free and the man went down choking out a strangled cry of agony. This time he wouldn't be getting up.

Jack tightened his grip on the other man's throat, placing the tip of the knife blade under the man's bearded chin. "The young doctor," he rasped, "where is he?"

The man shook his head wildly, so Jack increased the pressure, until a trickle of blood ran from under the man's chin, down his neck. The thug gasped, choked, then pointed at a large building lit by torchlight. Jack realised he'd been too busy to notice the impressive house that loomed behind him.

"Where in the house?" he growled, dragging the slaver to his feet, still holding the knife to his throat. The man shook his head again, and Jack figured he probably didn't know Mark's exact location. God alone knew what they were doing to him by this time. That thought made Jack see red, and he punched the slaver hard on the jaw, knocking him out cold. Using the rope he'd been tied with, he securely bound the unconscious man, shoved him under the truck out of sight, then did the same with the man he'd stabbed. *No need to tie him up, though.*

Shouldering the men's guns, he made his way to the house. *Where are you, Doc?*

* * * *

Mark stood silently while Omar and Hassan dressed him in the same style clothes they wore—a loose shirt and pants of some white, gauze-like material, and sandals.

The moment of reckoning, he thought, as Omar took his arm again with solicitous gentleness and led him to the door. This time, the armed guard accompanied them, following close behind as they made their way along the wide marbled corridor, then down the staircase to the grand entry hall. Mark had half expected to be met there by a sneering Malouf and possibly the man he'd been selected for, but the entry hall was empty, and the young men led him down another corridor until they reached a massive rosewood double door, where Hassan knocked twice, before pushing it open.

The sheer opulence of the room they entered made Mark gasp. His folks were wealthy and owned a couple of fairly large homes, but they faded to nothing in comparison to this magnificence. Every wall of the high-ceilinged cavernous room was covered in either exquisite tapestries or beautiful works of art. It looked like a collector's paradise.

Malouf and Fiqar, looking totally out of place, stood off to one side holding what looked like gold goblets. Fiqar smirked at Mark before raising the goblet to his lips and taking a sip of whatever it contained.

"Your Highness..." Malouf addressed the third person in the room, a tiny, withered old man dressed in a white robe and seated on a gold chair. "This is the young man we told you of. Quite a prize, would you not agree?"

The old man regarded Mark through eyes that were no more than slits in his wrinkled face. "Quite a prize, indeed," he said, his voice dry and cracked and barely audible. "Such lovely hair—Scandinavian?"

"An American, Highness," Malouf interjected. "An American *doctor*."

"An American doctor who's been taken here against his will," Mark snapped. "I suggest you quit this medieval crap, and let me go."

The old man smiled, his tongue flicking out to lick his lower lip. The move reminded Mark of a lizard, and he shuddered with repugnance. *If this old geezer thinks he's going to put a hand on me, he's out of his mind.*

"Come over here." The command, though no more than a whisper, was given in a manner that indicated the man expected to be obeyed.

Mark shook his head. "No, thanks."

"Doctor Hamilton," Malouf barked. "You will obey his Highness. He is Prince Rashid al-Ahmad, and right now, holds your very existence in the palm of his hand. It would be wise not to anger him." To emphasise his words, Malouf drew his gun and used it to wave Mark forward. "A bullet in the leg would be very inconvenient, no?"

Fiqar snickered as Mark reluctantly approached al-Ahmad. *Man, but I want a moment alone with you, Fiqar,* Mark seethed. *Just give me one chance to pop you on that stupid arrogant face…*

Prince Rashid al-Ahmad chuckled as Mark stood stiffly in front of him. He ran one withered hand up the inside of Mark's thigh and squeezed his balls. Mark jumped back, his face red with rage.

"Son of a —!" he exclaimed, swiping at the old man's hand. Simultaneous horrified gasps came from Omar and Hassan. Malouf growled then strode forward, ramming his gun into Mark's ribs.

"Down," he rasped. "Down on your knees before his Highness, American dog."

"Not on your life," Mark yelled. "You'd better shoot me now, because no way am I going to be this old guy's plaything. Oh, but wait, if you shoot me, you won't get your money, will you? What a dilemma, Malouf," he taunted the slaver. "Whatcha gonna do?"

A loud cackle had both Mark and Malouf staring at al-Ahmad. The old man's face was contorted with a kind of sinister amusement. He said something Mark couldn't understand, but it made Malouf grin.

Oh, oh, that's not good, Mark thought as Malouf's yellowed teeth appeared behind his thick lips.

"His Highness thinks that perhaps you need a lesson in humility, Doctor." He signalled to Omar and Hassan who moved forward, one on either side of Mark. Their gentle demeanour seemed to have been replaced with a certain roughness as they ripped Mark's shirt from him, then held his arms in surprisingly strong grips. Al-Ahmad rose shakily to his feet and took a step forward, a nasty smile twisting his almost invisible lips. He took Mark's right nipple between his thumb and forefinger, twisting it until Mark gasped from the pain. With his free hand he groped at Mark's balls, squeezing the sensitive sac in his claw-like grip.

"Ow! Jesus!" Mark yelled, struggling madly, kicking out at his tormentor. "Get off me, you fucking bastards!" The prince staggered back, a look of angry amazement on his face.

Whatever might have happened next was stalled as the massive doors were pushed open and two or three of Malouf's men spilled into the room. Mark could just make out the gist of what they were yelling, and his heart lurched with hope. Yes! Jack had escaped. He'd killed a guard, laid another one out, had taken their guns and was somewhere nearby.

"Jack!" Mark yelled at the top of his voice, before Malouf's sweaty hand clamped over his mouth.

"Find him," Malouf snarled. "Find him and kill him, now! Do not even think of bringing him to me alive." He thrust Mark towards Fiqar. "Watch him until we have found his friend and disposed of him." He bowed to the scowling old man who was being supported by Omar and Hassan. "Your Highness, my apologies for this disruption. I suggest you retire to safety until we have caught the interloper."

"My men will help you." al-Ahmad's voice was both angry and querulous. "And the American—next time, make sure he comes to me suitably tamed."

With a gun prodding the back of his skull, Mark was pushed from the room by Fiqar. The security commander held a tight grip on Mark's bare shoulder as they navigated the corridors until they reached a narrow staircase.

"Up," Fiqar said, giving Mark a shove forward, and reluctantly Mark climbed the steps ahead of him, thinking the whole time how he could take Fiqar by surprise. He'd wanted a moment alone with the jerk, and now, here it was... "Inside," Fiqar muttered behind him, moist lips too close to Mark's ear for his liking. Fiqar reached over Mark's shoulder and pushed open the door in front of them. Fiqar was so close now, Mark could feel the man's crotch brush his ass.

He's hard, Mark thought, with disgust — but that just might work to his advantage, and right now he was willing to try anything to get out of this mess and find Jack. He was sure Jack was close by. He had to be somewhere in the house by this time, and the fact no alarm had been sounded, no shouts or shots were echoing through the corridors, meant to him that Jack was still undiscovered, and doing what good soldiers do — tracking his prey — and hopefully, trying to find him.

Fiqar's hand brushed lightly down the length of Mark's spine, and he turned quickly, his face inches from Fiqar's. "You want me, don't you?" he whispered huskily. "I could feel you wanting me, your hard cock pressed up against my ass."

Surprised, Fiqar dropped his gun hand to his side, gasping as he felt Mark fondling his erection. He put his free hand behind Mark's head and pulled him in for a kiss. The queasy sensation of having Fiqar's tongue in his mouth made Mark want to throw up, but he swallowed his revulsion, pressing himself into Fiqar's body, his fingers sliding down the commander's arm until he could stroke the hand that held the gun.

"You won't need this," he murmured, slowly starting to pull the gun from Fiqar's grip. Fiqar almost fell for it, then some second sense must have kicked in. He pulled back to stare into Mark's eyes, his hand tightening round the butt of his gun.

Uh, oh... Mark brought his knee up into Fiqar's crotch, mashing his balls swollen with the lust that had flooded his blood only a moment before. Fiqar doubled over, screaming like a wounded animal, and Mark made the most of his advantage by wresting the gun from Fiqar, slamming it down on his head, then bolting from the room.

The sound of gunfire erupted from somewhere in the house, and Mark headed in its direction, hoping against hope he'd manage to stay out of the crossfire and get to Jack's side.

Jack was crouched behind a marble pillar, returning fire against Malouf's men. He figured they'd found reinforcements, probably the men employed by whoever owned this place. There had to be a dozen or so blazing away, and he thanked his lucky stars they were lousy marksmen. He'd already taken down two of them, their bodies sprawled on the floor of the huge entrance hall. That wasn't counting the two he'd surprised when he'd made his way into the house. *No sign of Mark, though, dammit*, he groused. *He could be anywhere in this fuckin' huge monstrosity. Just hope this ruckus'll slow down whatever they were planning to do to him.*

He could hear Malouf screaming orders over the almost deafening sound of Uzi's and AK47's. Bullets whined and ricocheted off the walls and statuary, sending marble chips and shards of glass flying everywhere. Suddenly, he was grabbed from behind. He felt the coldness of a steel blade at his throat. Only his razor-sharp instincts, honed over years of military training, saved him at that moment. Before his assailant could draw the blade across his throat, Jack brought his elbow up sharply, smacking the man under his chin, the hard muscle and bone of his elbow joint ramming into the man's Adam's apple. Gurgling and clutching at his throat, the man staggered backwards out from the pillar, exposing himself to the lethal gunfire that finished him off in seconds.

There was a momentary pause in the shooting as Malouf's men realised they'd killed one of their own, giving Jack a chance to reload. His eyes widened when he saw Mark appear in one of the corridors that led into the entry hall. Jack had just a moment to take in the fact Mark was bare-chested and wearing flimsy pants before the gunfire erupted again. He dove for cover, returning fire, praying Mark wouldn't try to make a dash for it across the entry hall.

Which was, of course, what he did. Jack cursed at the top of his voice as he saw Mark run towards him, then dive to the floor, rolling and crawling on his belly the rest of the way.

"God dammit, Doc," he yelled. Grabbing Mark by his hair he dragged him behind the pillar. "You want to get yourself killed?"

"Ow!" Mark yelled, shoving Jack's hands away from his hair. "And no, I don't want to get killed. Gimme one of those guns—"

"No chance," Jack snapped. "We're gettin' out of here. On three, keep your head down, and run like hell for the door. I'll cover you."

"What about you?" Mark demanded.

"I'll be right behind you. There's too many of 'em to hold off much longer. We'll stand a better chance if we can get to the first big truck right outside the door. I got the keys," he added. "Now, one...two...three!" He jumped up, sending a blistering volley into Malouf's gang, huddled behind pillars and various pieces of furniture. As he strafed the room with bullets, he was rewarded by the sounds of screams and the sight of Malouf's large body diving for cover. Jack bounded away, twisting his body to keep up his deadly stream of gunfire as he made for the door.

He could see Mark waiting by the truck. "Get in!" he yelled, leaping down the steps. He turned to send another burst of machine gun fire at the doorway and two of Malouf's men ran straight into the lethal barrage. Jack raced for the truck, threw himself into the cab, gunned the engine, then burned rubber, heading for the gates. "Closed," he muttered, staring ahead. "Fuck..."

"Ja-ack..." Mark's eyes widened as they drove straight for what looked like solid, immovable iron gates. "*Shit*...Jack!" he yelled, bringing his arms up to protect his face.

The truck hit the gates with a bone-jarring crash, then seemed to lurch sideways, catching one of the gates on the driver's side and tearing it free from the wall. Jack yelled in triumph as the gate fell away from the truck. He hit the accelerator hard, the truck fishtailed for a moment or two until Jack brought it under control, then they sped off into the blackness of the desert night.

Chapter Six

Jack glanced at Mark as the truck they'd stolen bumped and weaved on the rutted road. "You okay?"

Mark slumped back in his seat. "Amazingly, yes. I mean, what other doctor do you know who could honestly say he was just up for sale as a sex slave to a withered-up old member of some royal family? Who had to pretend he wanted to get into the pants of a man he found repulsive at best, just so he could try to make a break for it, then gets caught in the crossfire between a bunch of slave traders and one lone Australian sergeant major?" Mark paused to stroke Jack's thigh. "By the way, I still have to thank said sergeant major, in every possible way, and *position*, for saving my life—again."

Jack grinned at him. "Don't worry. I intend to exact payment soon as we shake those bastards."

Mark peered into the truck's side-view mirror. "Sons of bitches," he muttered, seeing wavering headlights behind them. "They're still after us…"

"Yeah, they won't give up easy." He handed Mark the AK47. "Know how to use one of these?"

"No, but this is a good time to learn."

"Try and hit the radiator. Don't aim for the driver. Radiator's an easier target. Wait 'til they get closer. I'd guess they have orders not to kill you. You're still a valuable item. Me, they'd liked to hang up by the balls. So, Doc, my life is in your hands."

Mark rolled down the side window and levelled the AK at the vehicle following them.

"Squeeze the trigger real gentle, and aim low. AK's got a kick 'til you get used to it."

"Gotcha," Mark muttered.

"I'm gonna slow down some, so they'll come up on us real fast. You ready?"

"Ready." Mark felt the drag of the truck's brakes, the headlights of the vehicle behind them suddenly looming closer. He pulled the AK's trigger and yelped as the butt smacked into his shoulder. His aim went high from the impact. "Shit!" He lowered the gun and pulled the trigger again. One of the headlights went out. "Yeah!" he yelled, firing again.

"You got 'im," Jack shouted. He could tell the vehicle had left the road, may even have gone over, but it was too dark to see for sure. What he could see was another set of headlights coming up fast behind them.

"There's another one," Mark said through gritted teeth. From the vague shape that he could see he guessed it to be the SUV Malouf had transported him in.

"Take 'im out," Jack yelled. "You've got the hang of it now."

Mark let rip with another burst from the AK. This time fire was returned, bullets whizzing past his head so close he could feel the heat. He fired again, shattering the SUV's windshield. The headlights became dimmer as the SUV lost speed. He must have either killed or injured the driver. Strange, he thought, that he felt no remorse.

"Good job." Jack gripped Mark's thigh as he fell back into his seat.

"Thanks." Mark took Jack's hand and laid it on his crotch. The adrenaline pumping through him had resulted in the erection that now strained the flimsy fabric of the pants Omar and Hassan had given him to wear. He turned to look at Jack through lust filled eyes. "Want you…" His voice was thick with emotion.

Jack grinned and gave the hard flesh between Mark's legs an appreciative squeeze. "Want you, too, and soon as I put enough space between us and those bastards, you're gonna find out how much."

* * * *

They drove through the darkness, Jack keeping his eye on his rear view mirror for any sign of lights behind them, but after about an hour he eased up on the gas pedal.

"Wish to Christ I knew where the hell we were," he muttered. "Bastards took everything — radio, compass — every damned thing I need." He flashed a grin at Mark "'Cept you, of course."

Mark eased himself over and rested his head on Jack's bare thigh. "You don't mind, do you?" he asked with a sensuous smile.

"Hell, no… just don't go playin' with the old fella down there or I might run us off the road."

Mark chuckled. "There's nothing old about this fella down here." He kissed Jack's prominent bulge. "But I'll be good 'til we find someplace I can let you take advantage of me."

The moon made a brief appearance overhead, shining through a mostly cloud laden sky, illuminating what passed for the road ahead, but also a large rock formation off to their right.

"What say we check this out?" Jack suggested. "We might be able to stay out of sight here 'til daybreak."

"Sounds like a plan." Mark peered at the immense outcrop of rock that rose from the desert floor like a giant fortress. "Looks like a castle was just dropped here," he murmured.

"It very well might serve as one, Doc."

Jack pulled off the road, then circled the rock formation until he found a place to hide the truck. He drove between two massive slabs of stone, and for a moment Mark had the strangest sensation they were entering some kind of citadel, a sanctuary where he and Jack would be safe, if only temporarily, from the dangers that had beset them since early that morning. The moon slipped out again from behind the clouds, casting long shadows on the rocks that surrounded them.

"What do you suppose this place is?" Mark whispered.

Jack shrugged. "Probably volcanic deposits. Let's take a look around." He indicated the glove compartment. "See if there's a flashlight in there."

Mark fumbled through the compartment and pulled out a long flashlight. He flipped the switch and grunted with satisfaction when a strong beam spilled out. Jack killed the lights, and grabbed the guns he'd taken from Malouf's men. They climbed out of the truck, standing together surveying what the flashlight's beam picked out.

"I think this might have been a refuge of some kind," Mark said. "Look, there's some kind of writing on that rock."

Jack chuckled. "Probably says 'abandon hope all who enter here' or somethin' like it."

"I don't get a creepy feeling from the place, do you?"

"No, can't say I do." Jack took Mark's hand and they walked deeper inside the rocky fortress, glancing up at the strange writings and occasional drawings they passed.

"You think it might have been a temple at some time or other?" Mark asked.

"Dunno. Don't know much about this kind of thing, really. What I'm wondering is if Malouf or that old geezer they were selling you to knows about it."

"Oh, right. But don't you think they'll have to wait until daylight to come looking?"

"Maybe. You slowed 'em down some when you took out both their vehicles." He put an arm around Mark's waist and pulled him in close. "You were ace back there. I was gobsmacked you could handle a gun like that."

Mark chuckled and turned to him willingly, pressing his bare chest to Jack's hard torso. "I *think* I understood what you just said…" Their lips met in a kiss that was gentle at first, then became feverish as desire rippled through their bodies.

"Let's go find somewhere I can take care of you," Jack muttered gruffly, when they finally came up for air.

"Right here will do..." Mark was unwilling to let Jack out of his arms. He nuzzled at Jack's nipples through the thin cotton of his tank top. "Take this off," he murmured, pulling at the top's hem. Jack slung the guns from his shoulders, laying them against one of the rock walls, then shucked off his tank top and stepped out of his shorts.

"Mmm..." Mark voiced his admiration, his eyes sweeping over the smooth musculature of Jack's torso, the fine dusting of black hair that covered his chest. "You are so fucking incredibly hot, Jack." He leant in again for another searing kiss that had his body trembling with desire and need. He wanted this man, wanted him more than he'd ever wanted or needed any other man in his life. He'd thought last night was to have been the only time he and Jack would have together—and now, to be here with him again, despite all the shit that had gone down in order for them to be here in each other's arms, Mark felt that given the choice, he wouldn't change one moment.

He licked his way from Jack's mouth, down the solid column of his throat, across his chest, lingering over each nipple, inhaling the scent of the man, a combination of sweat and musk and something that was uniquely Jack. He fell to his knees, his tongue sliding over the hard hot flesh of Jack's ridged abdomen, seeking the prize he knew jutted proudly from its thatch of curly black hair.

That prize he worshipped for a moment or two, gazing at its swollen, glistening head, at the slit oozing a translucent pre cum that tasted like salty nectar on the tip of his tongue. His eyes smiled up at Jack as he took him into his mouth. He pushed the foreskin back with his lips until the head was fully exposed, his tongue swirling over the crown, then up and down and around the hard-as-iron length with long hungry strokes. His hands caressed Jack's thighs, reaching round to cup his butt and pull him in deeper.

A ragged groan escaped Jack's lips and he forced himself to pull back from the sweet torture Mark was inflicting on him.

He pulled Mark to his feet. "I want to fuck you so bad," he growled.

"I want you to," Mark panted, unfastening the cord that held his pants tied around his hips.

"We don't have protection…"

Mark held Jack's concerned gaze, then said softly, "I'm negative. I've been tested scads of times…"

"Me too," Jack told him gruffly. "We get tested regularly — and you're the first bloke I've been with in months."

Mark grinned, his teeth gleaming in the moonlight that filtered through the rock fissures. "I didn't want to add that bit, but seeing as how you brought it up, it's been a long time for me too." He kissed Jack's lips gently. "And I'm glad it was you that broke the dry spell."

Jack's embrace tightened around Mark's lithe, naked body, and he lifted the smaller man into his arms. Mark wound his legs around Jack's hips, his arms around Jack's neck, while the big sergeant backed him up against the rock wall behind them, cushioning Mark's bare back from the rough stone by using the arm he supported him with. His shoulder muscles rippled from the effort of holding Mark in place, while he spat onto his fingers, then reached under Mark, lubricating the young doctor's eager hole with his saliva. Mark leant back in Jack's arms, positioning himself to give Jack access, then parting his butt cheeks with his hands, he lowered his ass onto Jack's throbbing erection, gasping as the hot hard flesh penetrated his still tender anus.

"Easy," Jack muttered, wanting Mark to dictate the pace.

"Oh, Jack..." Mark whispered on a quick intake of breath, his eyes wide and locked on Jack's.

"Don't want to hurt you," Jack murmured.

"No, no...it's good," Mark panted, winding his arms again around the big man's neck. "Mmm...really good...fantastic, Jack." He moved his butt up and down, drawing Jack's naked shaft deeper inside him with every gliding motion, the initial burning overcome by a wave of euphoria that seeped through Mark's blood, hardening his cock trapped between their torsos to an almost painful intensity. Jack now joined him, moving to the rhythm Mark had begun, thrusting upwards with long powerful strokes that soon had both men teetering on the edge of orgasm.

Their lips met in a kiss born of overpowering lust and need, their tongues plunging into one another's mouths, both of them lost in the sensual feel and the heat of each other's flesh. Sweat pooled between them as their bodies writhed together, and Jack's thrusts became longer, deeper. He groaned, burying his face in the crook of Mark's neck, biting down and sucking on the soft skin, branding Mark as his own.

"Ah, Jack—fuck me, man, fuck me!"

Jack's muscular body shuddered at Mark's moaning words. He tightened both arms around him and rammed himself inside Mark's heat harder, faster, until with a strangled cry of release he came in long, wrenching spasms of near painful pleasure. Mark stiffened in Jack's arms as he felt the hot surge of Jack's semen searing his insides. He let out a low moan of ecstasy as his cum shot between their sweat covered torsos, splattering onto Jack's chin.

Mark had never before felt so completely caught up in the act of sex. Yet here, held in the big Australian's arms, his chest still heaving from his almost unbearably exquisite climax, backed up against a wall of rock in the middle of only God-knew-where, in a physical position that might have had the writers of the Kama Sutra scratching their heads, he had never been happier. This almost animal coupling they'd just engaged in had for him become so much more than mere sex. So much more than a quick fuck under the stars with a hot Australian soldier...

"Jack..." His lips brushed over his lover's mouth. "That was amazing."

"Yeah, it was..." Jack moved into Mark's kiss then chuckled softly. "But I'm gonna have to put you down. My legs are cramping like billy-oh."

"Oh, sorry..." He moaned a little as Jack's cock slipped out leaving him with a feeling of emptiness, then he was pressed against Jack's hard chest again and his lips were taken in a long, slow kiss that had his head reeling all over again. If every night of his life ended as fantastically as this, he swore he'd put up with kidnappings and car chases just to get to this point!

Chapter Seven

"So, when are you goin' to tell me the reason you came to Darfur?"

The night had grown chilly and they'd retreated to the truck cab where Jack had sprawled on the bench seat, wrapping Mark in his arms, the doctor's back against Jack's chest.

"You really want to hear my bleeding heart story?" Mark wriggled his butt into Jack's crotch. "I can think of better things to do with our time."

Jack nibbled on Mark's ear. "You're a sex fiend."

"I know—ain't you the lucky one?"

"So, tell me anyway."

Mark sighed. "Okay, but let me warn you now, it's not pretty. The guy you're holding in your arms is a spoilt rich kid who led a fucked up life until his father gave him an ultimatum—shape up or ship out, without a penny."

"When you say fucked up, are you talkin' about drugs?"

"I'm talking about the whole enchilada—drugs, booze, parties in Mexico that got me and my friends all arrested. My father had to bail me out so many times from over the border—and let me tell you, you haven't lived 'til you've spent a couple of days and nights in a Mexican jail." Mark paused, remembering. "Oh, boy... Anyway, I can't really remember after what shit I'd gotten into, the old man said, 'That's it, Mark. Your mother and I are disgusted with you. We've spent a fortune on your education, you have a degree in medicine that you've done absolutely nothing with, so here's the deal...' And he told me I was no longer welcome in their home—*my* home—until I'd proved I could be someone other than the shit-faced loser he thought I was."

"So that's when you decided to join DCI?"

"Not exactly. What I decided to do was to show him I didn't give a damn about his pontificating. 'How dare you,' I yelled, 'threaten to throw me out?' We shouted at each other for about a half hour, then he had my mother try to talk to me, and God help me, Jack, but I was so rude and nasty to her. Even to this day, even though I've since apologised and she told me she loved me no matter what, I'm ashamed of what I said to that wonderful woman..."

"*Doc...*"

"I told you it wasn't pretty, and it gets worse. I stormed outta there and went on a three-day—or maybe four-day—binge, that amazingly didn't kill me. I woke up in some beach house in San Diego with a guy I didn't remember laying eyes on, never mind hands on. He was as wasted as me. The one good thing I realised later was we obviously hadn't had sex. I say good, because we had no protection, and I hadn't been tested in a while. Anyway, I spent the rest of the time in San Diego in the hospital suffering from alcohol poisoning.

"One of the doctors there kinda read me the riot act, and I don't know if it was because he was a total stranger, and not my mom and dad, that I found myself actually listening, and agreeing with what he was saying. When he found out I had a degree in medicine, he really went off the deep end. Called me all kinds of a loser, told me there were people all around the world looking for help, needing someone like me to give them medical attention, and *hope*...

"It was that last word that did it, Jack. *Hope*, for a better life, for someone who would actually care if they lived or died, and here I was shooting up and drinking myself into oblivion night after night, while those poor bastards wondered if they would see another day."

"It's sobering, that's for sure," Jack murmured, stroking Mark's chest.

"In more ways than one," Mark chuckled. "I stopped doing drugs, quit the bottle for over a year, and now I limit myself to just a social drink when the right occasion comes along – like with you and Harry."

"And that's when you joined DCI?"

"Not right away. The doctor who'd been yelling at me — Evan Richardson's his name — convinced me to apply for a job in that San Diego hospital. He and I became good friends..." He paused as he felt Jack's body tense under him. "*Friends*," he repeated, kissing Jack's cheek. "Did I sense a jealous twitch there?"

"No," Jack muttered.

"I did!" Mark laughed and turned over so he lay facing Jack. He rubbed his nose against Jack's. "Evan's a great guy, and cute, too." He laughed again at the sound of Jack's groan. "But, straight—married even, with *kids*."

Jack captured Mark's mouth with a long kiss, then bit down gently on Mark's full lower lip. "You always this much of a teaser?"

"Ow! And yes, Boomer, my boy, I love to tease big bad Australian sergeants just enough so I can get in their shorts, play with their big Australian uncut dicks and make 'em fuck me silly."

A deep chuckle rumbled through Jack's chest. "You're no shrinking fuckin' violet, that's for sure, Doc. And just how many of us Ozzies have you caught that way?"

"You're the first," Mark murmured, brushing his lips over Jack's. "I'd say you're the best, but then I have nothing to compare you with." Jack met his gaze full on, the piercing blue undimmed by the near darkness that surrounded them. "But then again, perhaps I won't ever want to compare..." He caressed Jack's right nipple with the palm of his hand, then squeezed it gently between thumb and forefinger. "I think you're too special to compare with anyone else..." He replaced his fingers with his lips, kissing the hardening nub, the tip of his tongue dancing over the tiny brown disc.

Jack tightened one arm around Mark's body; one hand gripped him by the hair on the back of his head, bringing their mouths together in a rough kiss that had Mark tasting blood. He ground his crotch into the hard bulge under Jack's shorts, and with a sigh of satisfaction, he gave in to the fierce desire that once again consumed him.

* * * *

"So, what about you, Jack?" Mark asked sleepily. His head rested on Jack's chest, his body suffused with the sheer boneless contentment of his sexual afterglow. "I've told you my darkest secrets and sordid past..."

"Don't have much of a sordid past," Jack said with a chuckle. "Pretty boring fella, really."

"That I don't believe." Mark nuzzled Jack's throat. "Did you volunteer to come out here?"

Jack stroked Mark's hair as he replied, "Yeah, glutton for punishment I am." His deep chuckle resonated in his chest. "After the government pulled us out of Iraq, I decided I wasn't quite ready to go home, so I volunteered for this duty. I've got another couple of months or so, then I'll head back to Oz."

"Got anyone waiting for you?" Mark teased, hoping the answer was a negative.

"Not any*one*, but I was left some land a few years back, so looks like I'll get stuck into doing what my da did for years, raise horses—there's a good market in Queensland. People like to ride, lots of room for it."

"Sounds like heaven," Mark murmured. "Very different from all this."

"Too right, it is. One thing I won't miss is all this bloody sand."

"I thought Australia was deserty."

"Not Queensland where I'm from. Pretty tropical actually, 'specially round the coast. You'd like it."

"Is that an invitation?" Mark asked through a yawn.

"Any time." Jack kissed the top of Mark's head and smiled at the sound of his gentle snore. He tightened his arms around the sleeping doctor and closed his eyes.

* * * *

The thrumming sound of a rotor engine overhead had Jack wide awake in seconds and leaping from the truck cab to scan the cloud-laden sky. A helicopter came into view, one he immediately recognised.

"Doc, quick!" he yelled, waving his arms wildly over his head. "They've found us. Get out here and jump about a bit!"

Mark rubbed his eyes as he climbed down from the truck. His muscles were stiff and sore from the cramped position he'd been lying in for the past few hours, and his ass burned from having Jack's hard cock up there — twice.

That was the good part, he thought, especially now they'd been found and he wouldn't see Jack again for God knew how long — maybe never. At least he had another night with Jack to remember, after they'd gone their separate ways. He joined Jack waving at the chopper, which dipped then straightened to let them know they'd been seen.

"Hey, Sarge!" Harry yelled as he jumped down from the helicopter. He took in Mark's state of undress with a raised eyebrow. "Somebody steal your clobber, Doc?"

"He means your clothes," Jack muttered.

"You could say that," Mark said, chuckling. "But I don't think I want to go back and get them."

"Saw a couple of abandoned vehicles off the road back there," Harry told them.

Jack nodded. "I'll make a full report when we get back to base. Where the hell are we, anyway?"

"About forty miles west of Khartoum. Quite a ways from Doc's clinic. How'd you get this far out?"

"Fuckin' slave traders," Jack growled. "Took him to some royal arsehole in place of Ghali, the kid you flew out along with the nurses."

Harry gaped at Mark. "They wanted to sell *you*, Doc?"

Mark grinned. "Hard to believe, isn't it? Never did see myself as somebody's sex slave."

"Too right," Harry agreed, obviously not wanting to get deeper into that particular conversation. "Anyways, let's get you on board. We'll find you some clothes at the base."

"It's okay to take me there?" Mark asked. "I thought it was kinda secret."

Jack chuckled. "Don't worry, you wouldn't find it again in a month of Sundays."

"Not the answer I particularly wanted to hear." Mark lowered his voice as Harry walked ahead of them. "What if I want to find *you* again?"

"What d'you mean, *if* you want to find me again?" Jack asked, punching Mark lightly on the arm. "You think you've got a choice here?"

"You mean you'll come visit me at the clinic?"

Jack stopped short, and grabbed Mark by the arm. "You're not going back there, Doc."

"Of course I am. That's where I'm needed, Jack. What I trained for—"

"But it's too fuckin' dangerous," Jack butted in. "You can't even trust the goddamn security patrol to protect you from rebels or slavers or any other arsehole who comes along."

Mark sighed, knowing this was going to be tough. "Jack," he said quietly, "this is what I signed on for. I can't just not go back. DCI depends on me to do my job, along with the patients who need help. I can't — *won't* — turn my back on them."

"Hey!" They both looked to where Harry was gesturing that they should get a move on. "You wallys comin' or what? Can't wait around here all day, y'know."

"We'll talk about this later," Jack muttered.

"Jack, there's nothing to talk about—"

"Later," Jack snapped. He strode towards the chopper and jumped on board. He held out a hand to help Mark, then pulled him against his chest and whispered close to his ear, "Later."

* * * *

"We took the kid and your patients to the base, Doc," Harry yelled above the roar of the rotors. He grinned as he added, "Paddy sure was happy that pretty nurse was there to look after him."

"You have medical facilities at the base?" Mark asked.

"Some," Jack told him. "Emergency stuff mostly. Anything serious we have to ship the guys to the UN hospital in Khartoum. Believe me, Paddy was lucky we were closer to your clinic."

Mark gazed down at the endless desert terrain spread out beneath him. Hard to believe that less than twenty four hours ago he'd almost been sold by Malouf and his gang of cutthroats to some ancient, dried-up prince with more money and time on his hands than was good for him. He shuddered to think what those two young men, Omar and Hassan, had to go through living under those conditions. But they'd been pretty keen to see him join their ranks, and not at all upset when al-Ahmad started fingering him. Still, what choice did they have?

At least Ghali had been spared that horror, and was now safely surrounded by UN soldiers. Maybe now the kid would have a chance at a decent life.

"What's going on in that mind of yours, Doc?"

Mark smiled at Jack. "Just thinking about Ghali, and thankful he didn't have to deal with what al-Ahmad had planned for him. It still makes me sick when I think what might have happened to him if you and Harry hadn't brought O'Brien in for treatment."

"It makes me sick when I think of what might have happened to you back at that old geezer's pad. Anyway, glad to have been of service."

Mark chuckled. "In more ways than one," he teased, noting with amusement that Jack's cheeks had coloured slightly under his tan. *Best change the subject*, he thought. "I'd like to find him a decent home if I could, especially if he can't go back to his parents."

Jack cleared his throat noisily. "They'd only sell him again. But we need to find out what the little fella wants to do." He pointed out the window. "There's the base."

Mark looked out at the sprawl of buildings, tents, and vehicles below him. "You have quarters there?" he asked.

"Yeah." He put his lips close to Mark's ear so Harry and the co-pilot couldn't hear. "You're invited, so I can talk you out of going back to that clinic."

"*Jack*, why are you doing this? I have no choice but to go back. I can't just leave the clinic unattended. DCI would probably kick my ass for...for dereliction of duty, or something."

"Okay, but I'm gonna make sure security gets beefed up around there, and that arsehole Fiqar gets arrested."

"If they ever find him," Mark said wryly. "You don't really think he'd show up back there do you?"

"Probably not, but you never know with someone like him. He's an arrogant enough wally to maybe think he can talk his way out of trouble. But if I see him again, he'd better run, and not look back."

"I kicked him in the balls twice." Mark grinned as the memory gave him a lot of satisfaction.

Jack frowned. "And don't think he'll forget that in a hurry."

Mark grimaced. "You're probably right. Well, I'll file a report when I get back, tell DCI exactly what happened, and make sure they know of Fiqar's involvement with Malouf..."

"Here we are then," Harry announced unnecessarily as the chopper landed with a thump amid a cloud of sand and dust.

"Thanks, Harry." Mark held out his hand to the pilot.

"No problem, Doc." He narrowed his eyes as he shook Mark's hand. "Those slavers do that to your neck?"

"Uh..." Mark rubbed the spot where Jack had bitten him. "Must have, I guess. I don't really remember."

"Oh, well...'spect the Sarge will find you some clothes."

"And a shower, I hope," Mark said, grinning.

"Come on," Jack growled, taking Mark's arm in his big hand.

"What did you do to my neck?" Mark asked, when they were out of earshot. He rubbed at it again. "Is there a bruise?"

"Yeah. Got carried away, didn't I? Sorry…"

"Don't be. Oh look, there's Ghali and Asima." He waved to his head nurse and the young boy standing at her side. Asima waved back then hurried to meet them, tugging Ghali along with her.

"Oh, Doctor Hamilton, I am so happy you are safe!" she cried, her dark eyes glistening. "Ghali and I have been so worried."

Mark gave her a quick hug, conscious of how he must look without his own clothes, then tousled Ghali's hair. "I have the sergeant major to thank for my rescue," he told them.

"Bad men are dead?" Ghali asked hopefully, taking Mark's hand.

"Some of them." Mark gave the boy's hand a gentle squeeze. "Let me get cleaned up and find some clothes to wear, then I'll tell you both all about my adventure."

Asima's eyes swept over Mark's bare chest, his bruised neck then down to the flimsy pants he wore. "Oh, Doctor, what did they do to you?"

Mark didn't want to tell her his present condition was more because of what Jack had done to him. "I…I'll tell you all about it later. Right now, I'm feeling a bit conspicuous."

He followed Jack over to a door in a prefabricated building. "This your digs, Digger?"

Jack gave him a raised eyebrow. "You're gettin' awful damn smart for someone who was almost somebody's fuck toy."

Mark grinned at him. "And instead I'm your fuck toy—"

Jack dragged him through the door, and slammed it shut behind them, "You are not my fuck toy," he growled, before fastening his mouth on Mark's. He broke off the kiss and scowled at Mark. "You got that? You're more than that to me—much more."

Mark was close to collapsing from the intensity of Jack's kiss. "Yeah," he said weakly. "I get that. But, Jack—"

"There's a shower in there. "Jack stepped back abruptly, pointing to a door in the corner of the room. "I'd join you but I have to go report to the field commander. I'll have Paddy bring you some clothes. Mine would be too big." He shucked off his shorts and grabbed a pair of khaki pants from the back of a chair. Mark was treated to the beautiful sight of Jack's muscular ass, then as he turned around, his thick cock, still impressive even when flaccid.

Mark's own cock hardened at the sight, tenting the almost sheer fabric of his pants. Jack's eyes narrowed as he watched Mark rub his erection enticingly. He looked up quickly at Mark's smiling face. "I'll be back in a jiff or two," he muttered, zipping up, "to take you to the mess tent. Now go shower."

"Yes, sir," Mark murmured, leaning in for another kiss. Jack gripped the back of his neck and held him in place while he scoured the inside of his mouth with his tongue.

"Mmm…more," Mark sighed.

"Can't keep the Major waiting, Doc." Jack sounded slightly short of breath as he pulled back. "I'll be back soon as I can."

"Damn." Mark watched him leave, then stepped out of the pants that now were not much more than rags. He looked around the room — *Jack's room*, he thought, smiling. It was small but tidy, with a single bed in the corner, flanked by a nightstand. A desk and chair were positioned in front of the window, facing out, a bureau with a stereo and some CD's on top completed the furnishings. Mark flipped through the CD's before turning his attention to a photograph beside the stereo. Jack, in the middle of a group of handsome men, smiled out at him, and there was no need for Mark to guess who the other men were. The likenesses were unmistakable. Jack's father and brothers...

Wow, so many of them. He counted six men, all but dear old Dad in army uniforms, though Mark would bet from his military stance he was a retired officer. So Jack came from a military family. Mark wondered where the brothers were deployed — and why there was no sign of Jack's mother in the picture. Deceased?

He walked into the bathroom and turned on the shower. *Hot water — my, the lap of luxury out here in Bumfuck, East Africa.* He stepped under the hot spray, and soaped himself vigorously. The soap stung his ass when he pushed his fingers in there. *No wonder, after the reaming Jack gave it.* His lips lifted in a small smile as he remembered their time together. Then he frowned slightly when he also remembered what Jack had said just before he'd left.

You're more to me than that — much more.

And yes, Jack meant more to Mark than just a hot cock up his ass. All his life, he'd avoided relationships.

Most of the time he'd been too fucked up to remember who he'd been with, and when he'd cleaned up his act he'd been too busy, and now—out here in the wilderness, where he'd least expected to find anyone he could remotely like, never mind have feelings for—

But it was impossible. Jack and him? Impossible.

We're poles apart, really. Jack out there, flying off on missions to godforsaken places, dodging rebel fire, trying to bring food and water to people suffering dire conditions—and me, stuck in a refugee camp clinic, for now anyway, until the mucky mucks at DCI decide to transfer me—if ever...

Impossible—and way too soon to be thinking long-term relationship.

Mark rinsed himself off, then grabbed a towel from the rail by the shower stall. Jack could maybe come to see him from time to time, but how would he explain that to his men? Surely they didn't know Jack was gay? And how would they react if they caught on? Not that he was worried about Jack having to defend himself.

That guy could take on a grizzly and most likely knock it cold.

Mark chuckled at the thought. Still, he wouldn't want to see Jack lose face among his men. He had sensed a real camaraderie between Jack, Harry and Paddy. Good friends—friends who would defend each other no matter what. *No matter what*? Well, some things, some phobias, were insurmountable, and he'd hate like hell to see Jack hurt in any way by what knowledge of their relationship might do. Of course, he reminded himself, he was putting his American mindset on this. Gays had been allowed to serve in the Australian military for a number of years, so it could very well be that his men knew all about Jack's sexuality, and had no problem with it.

He was brought abruptly from his thoughts by a sharp knock at the door. He wrapped the towel round his hips and padded from the bathroom. "Who is it?" he yelled.

"Paddy O'Brien, Doc. Brought you some clean clothes."

Mark swung the door open. "Hi, Paddy. Come on in." He glanced at the bandage visible under Paddy's shirt. "How's the shoulder?"

Paddy shrugged without too much difficulty. "Almost good as new, thanks to you." The young soldier's eyes were glued to the bruise on Mark's neck. "Heard you had a rough time of it after we left," he said, handing Mark a bundle of clothing.

"You could say that. Thanks for these." Mark grinned at O'Brien. "Nothing quite like being treated like an animal at auction to give you a new perspective on life."

"Just as well the Sarge was there with you."

Mark nodded. "Yes." He found a shirt in the bundle and slipped it on. "Whose clothes am I borrowing?"

"Mine, Doc. Sarge figured me and you were about the same size."

"Well, thanks, Paddy. I'll look after them and return them soon as I can."

"No problem, Doc. They're army issue. So...did you get bit there, on your neck?"

Mark hoped he wasn't blushing. He turned away to throw his towel to one side and slip on a pair of khaki shorts. "Uh, actually, I'm not sure how that happened," he lied. "So much was going on with the slavers, the guys I was being sold to, Jack coming in, guns blazing. It could have happened any time, you know." He zipped up the shorts and faced Paddy again. "I'm just grateful Jack was there, and that Harry showed up this morning."

Paddy seemed satisfied with Mark's explanation. Mark sat on the bed and pulled on a pair of socks that had been tucked inside the army boots Paddy had brought. He tried a boot for size.

"Not bad," he muttered, then looked up and smiled at Paddy. "Lucky for me, our feet match too."

Paddy grinned. "Not mine. Asima told me your size."

"You like her, don't you?"

"Yeah, she's a cracker and no mistake. Been looking after me like I was somebody special."

"All patients are special, Paddy. Asima's one of the best nurses I've worked with."

Paddy nodded. "Right, Doc, I'll be off. Sarge'll be here soon as he can to take you to the mess for some grub. Hoo-roo, then. See you later. "

"Yeah, later, Paddy." *Hoo-roo?* Who knew? Chuckling, Mark went back into the bathroom to clean his teeth. He wondered if Jack would mind him using his toothbrush. *Better not, without asking, no matter where my mouth has been*, he thought, grinning to himself. He squeezed some toothpaste onto his finger and rubbed it over his teeth and tongue. *A-ah, minty breath at last. Just right for one of Jack's hot kisses.*

He paused, examining the bruise on his neck where Jack had marked him. A love bite. Again, the memory of Jack's hot body pressed to his sprang into his mind, the way they'd cleaved together out there in that strange hideaway they'd stumbled into, the feel of Jack's big, hard cock moving in and out of him—Jeez!

J.P. Bowie

Chapter Eight

He jumped as the door flew open and Jack barged in, like the proverbial bull in the china shop. "Goddamn pissin' bureaucratic horse manure," he yelled at Mark who stared at him wide-eyed.

"Jack, what the hell's the matter with you?"

"Fuckin' wallys at the UN are tellin' us we have to stand down until further notice 'cause some government arsehole in Khartoum has complained we're too *aggressive* on our patrols. I'll give them aggressive," he fumed, punching the palm of one hand with his fist.

"Jack, calm down, and tell me what happened." Mark stepped forward, put his arms around Jack's waist and kissed him on the lips.

"Mmpf..." Jack dragged his mouth across Mark's, his arms coming up to crush Mark in an angry embrace. "Bastards," he mumbled finally, pressing his forehead to Mark's. "Sorry...don't mean to yell at you.

It's not you, it's just every other fuckin' thing they throw at us around here."

"What is it, Jack?" Mark asked softly. "Come sit on the bed, and tell me…"

Jack sighed but let Mark lead him to the narrow bed where they sat side by side, their arms around one another.

"The day I brought Paddy to you for treatment," Jack began slowly, "I think I told you we'd been under fire from rebels while we were delivering goods to the village. We returned their fire, but me and the lads are always careful to avoid collateral damage. I would swear on the memory of my mother that we didn't hit any civilians, but now I'm told two children were killed in the crossfire. Children, Mark… They sent pictures of the bodies…" Jack's breath shuddered in his chest, and he fell silent for a few moments.

Mark pressed himself to Jack's body and kissed his cheek. Somewhere in the midst of his wish to comfort the big Australian, he had the realisation that Jack hadn't referred to him as 'Doc', but for the first time since they'd met, had called him Mark.

"Do you think that maybe the rebels killed the kids then put the blame on you?" he asked quietly.

Jack shrugged his broad shoulders. "It'd be the typical crap they like to pull, but the UN hierarchy have to kow-tow to the Sudanese government, or at least pay lip service."

"When you say, 'stand down', what does that mean exactly?"

"It means no more missions 'til the order's rescinded. And that means the rebels will be out there terrorizing anyone in reach, and we can't do a bloomin' thing about it."

"What about the other peacekeeping forces — the US and the Brits?"

"Dunno, but it's a pretty safe bet they'll be under restrictive orders. Pisses me off, Doc. It gives the rebels a firmer grip on the territory. They'll be all over the place with no one to curtail their activities."

Mark, wanting to ease Jack's frustration, slipped a hand inside Jack's shirt, stroking his chest and laying gentle kisses on his neck.

Jack groaned. "You're tryin' to take my mind off all this, aren't you?"

"Is it working?"

"Almost…"

Mark fell back on the bed, pulling Jack down on top of him, grinding their crotches together. "How's this?" he murmured.

"Getting better every minute."

Mark felt Jack's grin against his lips. He pulled Jack's shirt free of his pants and caressed the smooth muscular back underneath.

"I should shower," Jack mumbled into Mark's mouth.

"No time for that…" Mark drew back a little, his eyes gleaming. "But please tell me you have some lube."

"That I have, but you're not puttin' that pretty mouth of yours anywhere near my privates 'til after I've showered. And that's an order." Before Mark could protest, Jack rolled off of him and headed for the bathroom. "Be with you in a jiff," he said over his shoulder. "Don't go startin' without me!"

"Like I would." Mark chuckled. "It wouldn't be quite the same, now, would it?" He lay back on the bed, then wriggled out of the shirt and shorts he'd been provided with. Listening to the sound of the shower spray, he imagined the water coursing over Jack's muscles, his hands spreading the shower gel across his chest, brushing over his nipples, bringing them to small hard nubs of sensitive flesh, positively aching for Mark's lips...

"Oh God," he groaned, gripping his burgeoning erection. "Hurry up, Jack." He heard the twist of the faucet turning off the water.

"You say something out there?"

"No..." Mark stared guiltily at his hard cock arcing over his flat stomach.

Jack appeared in the bathroom doorway. "Naughty boy," he scolded. "I said no starting without me, and look at that big fella there."

"He's happy to see you." Mark grinned up at him.

Jack threw aside the towel he'd been running over his hair, then knelt by the side of the bed. "I'm happy to see him too," he murmured. "Mmm..." His tongue swiped over the head, licking at the copious pre cum gathered on the slit.

Mark let out a long, shuddering breath at the touch of Jack's lips and tongue on his heated flesh, then writhed when Jack cupped his balls, squeezing each one gently, causing ripples of erotic pleasure to course through Mark's body.

"Get on top of me," he whispered urgently. "Wanna feel all of that hot body on mine."

Jack obliged, easing his muscular frame onto the bed, then pulling Mark into his arms. Their bodies meshed, rock hard cocks sliding over one another, pre cum mingling on their bellies. Mark wound his legs round Jack's hips, raising his butt, opening himself to the bigger man, his green eyes now locked on Jack's, darkened by a wanton lust he could barely control.

"Jack," he murmured on an exhaled breath, "you are so fucking amazingly sexy..."

His words were stifled by Jack's mouth taking his in a long, demanding and hungry kiss that sent Mark's senses into overload. Jack's tongue swept inside his mouth, filling every corner with its sensual caresses. He wrapped his arms around Jack's neck holding him in place while their lips meshed in kiss after bruising kiss, and their bodies melded together, chest to chest, and cock to cock.

Mark moaned his need into Jack's mouth. "Fuck me, Jack, I need that big, beautiful dick of yours inside me. Give me something to remember when I'm alone again..."

Jack growled and reached a hand inside his nightstand drawer, pulling out a tube of lube. He raised himself and knelt between Mark's thighs, his eyes raking over the young doctor's body with undisguised desire. He squeezed some lube into the palm of his hands then rubbed them together to warm the lube before taking hold of Mark's erection and his own, massaging them together in his slick hands. Mark gazed up at him with something akin to worship in his eyes, but in their green depths Jack could see lust, and want, and need — and he felt a quickening in his chest, an ache and a longing he had never before experienced with another man.

"*Mark...*" He marvelled at the almost choked-off sound of his own voice, so full of the emotional desire the younger man imbued him with. He leant in to take Mark's mouth in another long, searing kiss, at the same time pressing his lube slicked fingers into

Mark's quivering hole. "Okay?" he murmured, aware the rough sex they'd indulged in the night before might still leave Mark sore and tender.

A soft whimper escaped from Mark's throat as he raised his hips to accept Jack's exploring fingers. "Yes," he whispered, his lips on Jack's, their breath mingling as the head of Jack's cock replaced his fingers, easing past Mark's yielding resistance. Jack gasped, feeling Mark's tight hole enclose him in its silky heat, drawing him in, letting him lose himself in his own carnal need. He started slow, holding Mark's body, rocking to a gentle rhythm that gained strength and impetus with each successive push from Jack's powerful pelvis. Mark was moaning now, his arms and legs wound around Jack's torso pushing himself forward to meet every thrust from Jack's cock.

"Jack...*Jack*..." Mark's suddenly so young and trembling voice, filled with passion and need murmuring in his ear, his warm sensuous lips moving over Jack's fevered skin, drove the big Australian wild with an almost uncontrollable lust. His rhythm quickened as his own need took over and he plunged ever deeper into Mark's hot, sweet asshole. Mark writhed under him, his ass muscles tightening their grip on Jack's cock, his moans of pleasure mixed with pain filling Jack's ears, bringing him closer and closer to the edge. He grasped Mark's straining erection in his big hand, using the pre cum that spilled over his fingers as lubricant, pumping the pulsing shaft in time to his own deep thrusts.

His orgasm roiled in his balls. He gasped out loud as he soared beyond all control, plunging one last time into Mark's core, his cum surging up the length of his cock, exploding inside Mark with an intensity that had

Jack seeing stars. From somewhere he heard Mark's stifled cry of ecstasy, warmth coated his fingers and chest, then his mouth was captured in a kiss that made him come again, and again.

"Holy shit..." Mark's breathy exclamation followed by a deep chuckle brought Jack out of the haze that clogged his brain. The young doctor's soft lips trailed across the stubble on Jack's cheek and his sigh was one of deep contentment. "Jack...you are without a doubt the best in all the world."

Jack grunted and tightened his arms around Mark's lithe body, pushing his still-hard cock into Mark's heat. "Takes two, y'know," he mumbled into the crook of Mark's neck.

"Mmm...love you inside me, Jack. Stay there all day, please."

"Much as I'd like to, we have things to do."

"Nothing as terrific as this."

"True." Jack eased himself out of Mark and sat up. When Mark complained he pulled him into his arms and silenced him with a long kiss.

"Tell me we get to do this again before I have to leave," Mark whispered against Jack's lips.

"*If* you leave..."

"*Jack*."

"Okay, okay...we'll talk after we've had some grub. Come on..." He stood, pulling Mark to his feet. "Need to shower again after all that..."

Mark gave him a teasing smile. "There's room for two in there."

"But can I trust you to behave yourself?"

"Absolutely not."

Jack grinned. "That's what I thought."

* * * *

Harry and Paddy, along with Asima and Ghali were seated in the mess tent when Mark and Jack finally got there. Mark had to admit he was starving, and the smell of roast chicken made his mouth water and his stomach rumble, reminding him he hadn't eaten since the previous morning. Despite his hunger pangs, he was quick to notice that Ghali looked so much more at ease now. Perhaps the nightmares that had plagued the boy would finally be replaced by peaceful sleep. He grinned at Ghali, and was touched when the boy ran to him, and by his reaction when he knelt down to give him a hug.

Ghali's arms wound around Mark's neck. "Ghali is happy bad men did not keep you."

"I'm real happy about that too," Mark said with a quick grin. "So, you like being here, Ghali?"

Ghali nodded, taking his hand and tugging him over to where Asima sat, a big smile on her pretty face. "Doctor, you look so much better now."

"Amazing what a shower and clean clothes can do for a guy," Mark quipped.

"Let's get some grub." Jack grabbed him by the arm. "You can gab later."

"You always this bossy?" Mark asked as they made their way to where the steaming pans of food were lined up.

"Yes," Jack growled. "And now that I won't have any of my men to order around for a bit, I'll just have to pick on you."

"Until I go back to the clinic."

"Yeah, about that…"

"Don't start again, Jack. Tomorrow morning, I'd be grateful if you'd arrange some kind of transportation for me."

"We'll talk about it."

"*Jack*. We've already talked about this."

"No, we haven't. We were goin' to, then you got me all distracted back there, and it sort of slipped my mind." He gave Mark a sly grin. "Nice distraction though."

"You are incorrigible, Sergeant Major Boomer." Mark picked up a plate and began heaping chicken and potatoes onto it. "I really need to get back there, if only to make sure the rebels haven't taken advantage of the situation the slave traders created, and to also make sure that bastard Fiqar isn't reinstated as security commander."

"Right," Jack agreed piling his food plate high. "I'll talk to the CO and see if I can get us a chopper. What about Asima?"

"I'll ask her if she wants to go back with me, but if she doesn't I can ask DCI to transfer her somewhere else."

But as they sat at the table Asima immediately asked Mark when they would be going back to the clinic. Mark met Jack's eyes for the briefest of moments before he replied, "Thank you, Asima. I'm going back tomorrow, but I'll completely understand if you'd rather not."

"Oh no, Doctor, we are needed there," Asima said firmly. "Fatima and I are ready whenever you are. We talked about it earlier today. We can't let rebels or other bad men scare us away. The people need us – and, especially you."

Ghali stared at them with frightened eyes, so Mark took his hand and squeezed it gently. "Don't worry, Ghali, you will stay here with the soldiers until we can arrange something more permanent for you."

"Do you have a family?" Jack asked the boy.

Ghali nodded, but tears glistened in his eyes. "My mother was killed last year, and my father—" He broke off and tried to swallow the sob that threatened to escape his throat. "He told me he could not afford to keep me, and that I would have a better life if he sold me."

"Bastard," Jack muttered under his breath. Louder, he added, "Well, don't fret, young cobber, we'll make sure you don't have to go back there."

Ghali lifted his gaze to Mark. "I don't want any of you to go back. Stay here with me. It's safe here."

Mark smiled at the boy. "We have to go, Ghali. The patients need us there, but don't worry, I'm sure the men who took you from your father are many miles away by now."

Ghali looked far from convinced, but said no more as everyone ate their lunch. Mark could tell by the look on Paddy's face that the young soldier was not happy either. He kept shooting worried glances at Asima. It was obvious he had feelings for her, and Mark wondered how that could possibly play out. They had as many obstacles to overcome as he and Jack did, perhaps more, for Paddy didn't have the privileges Jack did. He didn't have the rank to request a helicopter or transport truck from the CO. Mark made a mental note to ask Jack to make sure Paddy accompanied them to the clinic in the morning.

Back in Jack's quarters, Mark asked, "You think the CO will okay you taking us back to the clinic?"

Jack nodded. "He already has. Major Holbrook's an easy-going bloke, and as pissed as me about the new orders. Besides, he's not going to let you find your own way, now, is he?"

Mark chuckled. "Not unless he wants a doctor and his nurses staggering about in the desert, lost and withering away from lack of water."

Jack grimaced. "What I don't want is you and your nurses there alone, after we have to leave."

Mark didn't want that either, but telling Jack that would be tantamount to starting their argument about him not going back to the clinic all over again. "We'll be fine, Jack. You can check in with me every day if you like. I promise to answer every call."

"You'd better," Jack growled, pulling Mark into his arms.

Teasingly Mark added, "If I'm not too busy," then brushed Jack's lower lip with his own.

"Bugger that," Jack murmured, opening to Mark's probing tongue. Their kiss was long and sweet, each man savouring the taste and scent of the other.

"Oh, Jack..." Mark sighed when the kiss ended. "What am I going to do without you close to me all the time? We've known each other for such a short time, but already I feel you're a part of me I don't want to let go."

Jack's hands roamed over Mark's body, slipping under the waistband of his shorts to caress the round swell and smooth skin of his ass cheeks. "My tour's up in less than a couple of months," he said, his voice low and husky. "I'm not signing up again. Had it in my head to go home. You could come with me..."

"To *Australia*?"

"Would it be so bad?" Jack loosened his embrace and leant back to look into Mark's eyes. "It's a bloody good country, you know."

Mark smiled and kissed Jack's lips. "I'm sure it's wonderful. It's just that I never saw Australia in my future before. I hadn't much thought of where I'd go after Darfur."

"Well, now you have something to think about. Australia with me."

"What about your parents, and brothers?"

Jack's eyes clouded for a moment. "Mum died some years ago when I was just a kid – cancer."

"I'm sorry."

"It was a long time ago. Kept Da busy though, looking after all us lads."

"And does he know about you – that you're gay? Won't he and your bros mind you bringing a gay man home?"

Jack chuckled. "There's five of us, two of us like fellas. My brother Sam, he's the youngest, he's gay same as me, got himself a nice fella. The other three are all married, got a brood of kids long as my arm, can't remember their ruddy names half the time. Anyway to answer your question – no, they won't mind me bringing you home. 'Sides, I have my own place..."

"And your Dad?"

"He's not gay," Jack said, with a deadpan expression.

Mark laughed softly. "Idiot." He kissed Jack's mouth with a gentle brush of his lips. "I meant, how does he handle all of this?"

Jack cupped Mark's face between his big hands and kissed him back. Then he slid an arm around Mark's waist and steered him over to the bed.

"Oh good," Mark exclaimed, "we're going to have sex again."

"After we finish our chinwag." Jack pulled Mark down onto the bed and wrapped his arms around him.

"You know this is no position for conversation," Mark complained. "How can I concentrate when all I can feel is your hot body pressed against me, and your hard dick trying to get into my ass."

"It's not going into your arse — yet," Jack growled. "Now listen up…"

"Yes, sir." Mark smiled and turned to kiss Jack's chin. "You have my complete attention — "

"Cheeky bugger." Jack nipped Mark's earlobe with his teeth. "You asked me about how my dad handles having gay sons — well, it might surprise you to know he's the one that pushed Sam into the relationship he has with Ronnie, his fella."

"You're kidding!"

"No. Dad met him at some charity do for veterans in Brisbane. Ronnie's dad was killed in Vietnam. He was a speaker at the function and Dad went to chinwag with him after, sussed he was gay, so he invited him over for dinner when Sam was home on leave — and that was that."

"Wow." Mark tried to envisage his own father setting him up with a guy, and couldn't quite see it. "Has he ever tried setting you up with a guy?"

Jack's deep chuckle vibrated through Mark's back. "Not yet — well, now he won't have to, will he?"

Mark was silent for a moment or two, digesting what Jack had just told him, then he turned in Jack's arms and met his piercing blue-eyed gaze. "Jack...are we rushing things a bit? We've only known each other for a few days, and—"

Jack's face stiffened slightly. "Just a few minutes ago you were saying you didn't know how you'd cope without having me around, now you're stalling. So, Doc, what's it to be?"

"You don't have any doubts?"

Jack sighed. "'Course I have doubts. Like you said we hardly know each other, but something, I don't know what, something inside me tells me this is right. It's not just the sex either, though that's fuckin' brilliant..." His eyes locked on Mark's, and his smile was almost shy and boyish. "Well, isn't it?"

"Yes, it is, Jack," Mark murmured. "The best sex I've ever had in my life." He grinned at his lover. "You're a tiger between the sheets."

"Too right—and you're not so bad yourself, mate." He chuckled, then tightened his arms around Mark. "But you're right, I reckon, about me rushing things. Sort of a habit of mine. When I want something, I grab it with both hands."

Mark nuzzled Jack's neck, kissing the stubbled warm skin, inhaling his masculine scent. "You can grab me with both hands anytime you like."

Those hands slid down Mark's back to cup his butt, squeezing each cheek, pulling his crotch into Jack's hard bulge. "You'll think about it, though? Give Australia a shot with me, I mean, when all this is over?"

"Yes," Mark whispered. "And thank you, Jack. I'm...honoured that you asked me."

Nowhere to Hide

Chapter Nine

Two weeks later

Mark looked up from the wound he was examining and caught Asima's eye. The elderly woman he was treating had been beaten by two men when she'd refused to share what little food she had. One of them had cut her arm with a knife, an obviously dirty knife, from the look of the infection that had turned the cut an angry red round the edges, and from the amount of pus that had gathered deep inside.

"Asima, let me have the antibiotic solution, please."

He had already thoroughly cleaned the wound with disinfectant and drained out the pus. He took the gauze soaked with the antibiotic solution Asima handed him and gently pushed it into the wound. He stood aside as Asima took over, bandaging the woman's arm all the while softly saying words of encouragement to her. Mark was always astounded at the stoicism of the people he treated. With very few exceptions, they remained silent and uncomplaining even when what he was doing sometimes caused them pain.

A vibrating at his waist made him smile. He detached the cell phone from his belt and flipped it open. "Hello, Jack." The phone was courtesy of the Australian military with a signal powerful enough to connect him with Jack's base camp.

"Hi, Doc. How's it goin' down there?"

Jack's husky voice made Mark's toes curl and his groin ache with need. God, how he missed this man. "Fine," he replied. "Same as yesterday and the day before. The clinic's filled to capacity again, and the motherfuckers in charge haven't been anywhere near since you left. It's like they didn't even know we'd been gone for three days."

"You talked about getting transferred yet?"

"No, Jack, not yet."

"When?"

"Soon, Jack, I promise. I just want to look after these people until the government gets some kind of permanent care for them."

"But that might take months, *years*," Jack growled.

Mark sighed. They'd had this conversation before, and it always ended in both of them showing their frustration.

"Sorry, Doc, sorry..." Jack had heard Mark's exasperated sigh. "I'm being pushy again. I just worry about you being there. I can't get out your way 'cause they have us back on regular missions as of today. I'm flying to Dakran in about an hour. I'll try and keep in touch, but don't know if the signal will be strong enough to reach you."

"How long will you be gone?"

"Dunno. Long as it takes — three, four days I expect. Something to do with the elections they're gearing up for."

A pang of unease settled in Mark's stomach. News of riots and civil disobedience had been rife since the elections were announced. Even in this remote refugee camp, officials were being trucked in to inform the people they must vote. Not one of those officials had come near the clinic.

"Be careful, Jack."

"'Course I will. I'll try phoning, but if you don't hear from me, you know the reason why. Gotta go, Doc. Take care."

"You too, mate."

Jack chuckled as he hung up. Damn, Mark was beginning to hate every moment he was apart from Jack. He never could have guessed he'd miss the man so much. Missed his gruff yet gentle demeanour, his quiet strength, even his sometime tendency towards bossiness, he reflected with a wry smile. He missed all of that, and in the nightly solitude of his tent, he missed him most of all. Missed his big, warm, strong body that could be so surprisingly tender, his big hands, his big feet, his big — *Okay, that's enough of that,* he told himself, realising he was getting hard. *Not here, Mark, and not in front of Asima and the patients!*

A letter was delivered to him later that day, from his parents. Mark took it to his tent to read, grimacing as he glanced at the postmark. It had only taken four weeks to reach him! What the hell had they used — camel post?

The letter, written mostly by his mother, with a postscript from his dad, made him feel even more remote from everything and everyone he knew. Not for the first time he wondered how long it might be before he'd get home to see them again. If he moved to Australia… That possibility had been a constant in his mind ever since Jack had first broached the subject. How would his folks take that news? Their only son trekking off to the other side of the world to raise horses with a guy they'd never met, never even heard of. They would have to have a family reunion somewhere in the bush… The thought made him smile.

He didn't hear the soft footfall behind him, nor the almost silent rustle of the silk-like material that suddenly covered his face. He inhaled once sharply from the shock, and that was all it took. His vision blurred, his legs went to jelly under him and he pitched forward, saved from thumping his head on the hard ground by the powerful arms that held him. He was only dimly aware of voices, muttering, ordering – then everything went black.

* * * *

Jack peered down at the village beneath him as the supply helicopter carrying him and his men hovered over the random collection of shacks and mud-walled buildings. It looked deserted, yet he'd been told there were people here in need of food and water. As it was on the route to Dakran, they'd been given the job of delivering the much needed supplies on the way to the larger town.

"Take her down for a closer look," he told Harry, using his binoculars to scan the area below them. "There, look…" His men stared at the group of men, women and children that had emerged from the buildings. One of the children gave a tentative wave. "Poor blighters," Jack muttered. "Okay, Harry, take her in…"

Less than an hour later, they were again airborne and heading for Dakran. Jack couldn't quite get the images of the dirt-poor people they'd left behind out of his mind. More and more, these scenes of abject misery, inflicted on the people by rebels and government alike, were getting harder for him to take. He'd thought after his tour of duty in Iraq, he'd seen it all. The danger from suicide bombers, rival factions and insurgents filled the everyday life of the Iraqi people with nerve-racking tension and uncertainty. But at least the majority of people had fairly decent homes and access to food and water, while here, a mere existence was almost impossible to scrape from the unforgiving terrain. Without the sometimes erratic help provided by teams like his, these largely forgotten people would perish.

He knew it wasn't a good idea to dwell on this too much. There wasn't a whole heap more he, or any other outsider, could do for them without the direct cooperation of the country's government, and certainly not with the amount of restrictions placed on the UN by the very people they were trying to help. Still, it burned him up inside when he saw the desperate plight of the victims of this terrible and seemingly never-ending conflict.

"You okay back there, Sarge?" Harry's voice broke into his reverie.

"Yeah, yeah." Jack stretched his long body and stared out the window at the endless vista of scrub and sand below. "How much longer we got?"

"Another hour or so. You were being awful quiet."

"Thinking."

"Thought I heard a funny noise."

"Ha, ha." He looked out the window again. Something was moving across the desert floor. He pulled out his binoculars for a better look. "Shit," he muttered as an armed vehicle came into focus through the lens. "Harry, rocket launcher to starboard. Better take her up."

"Roger that," Harry replied tersely. The six other men in Jack's contingent, including Paddy—now fully recovered from his shoulder wound—came to full alert.

Jack trained his binoculars on the vehicle travelling the road beneath them. It appeared as though the men on board were oblivious to the helicopter, the noise of their own engine probably drowning out the 'copter's.

"Doesn't look like it's us they're after," Jack muttered.

"Who then?" Paddy asked, leaning over Jack's shoulder to peer through the window.

Jack scanned the area ahead of them. "See anything, Harry?"

"Not yet…wait…about three clicks ahead. Dust cloud of some kind."

Jack rose from his seat and stood by his pilot, binoculars focused on the desert road in front of them. "Yeah, I see it…could be some kind of transportation, lorries maybe. Stay behind those blighters with the rockets. Let's see what they're up to."

It didn't take long to figure it out. As they came in range of the dust cloud Jack could see two open-sided trucks filled with people. "Damn," he muttered. "They must be taking them into Dakran for the election."

"And those bastards down there are out to stop them," Harry said, his grip tightening on the controls. "What'll we do, Sarge?"

Jack watched as two men who'd been riding in the back of the truck started preparing the rocket launcher for firing.

"Time to let them know they don't exactly have it all their way," Jack replied. "Take her down, Harry. We'll give them a warning burst. See if that puts them off their stride a bit."

Harry took the 'copter lower, circling the armed vehicle then firing a burst from the chopper's guns, kicking up the sand in front of the truck. Obviously taken by surprise, the truck veered off the road, skidding and bumping over the loose sand for several yards before the driver regained control.

"They're returning fire!" Paddy yelled as the two men raised what looked like Uzis and took aim at the helicopter.

"Bugger that," Jack muttered, sliding the 'copter door open and levelling his AK47 at the truck. The men on the truck dove for cover as the bullets from his gun peppered the side of the vehicle. Then one of them, hiding behind the rocket launcher itself, cranked the mechanism, turning the launcher to take aim at the helicopter.

"Shit," Jack hissed, getting the top of the man's head in his sights. There was no time for him to weigh the rights and wrongs of this situation. The men below were out to kill innocent civilians, and Jack and his crew along with them if he didn't stop it now. Hang the consequences. He squeezed off another shot, and grunted as the man was slammed backwards off the side of the truck. The other man tried to take over but was hampered as the truck bucked and shuddered over the rough ground trying to get back on the road.

"Circle back round again, Harry," he yelled. "Try shooting out the tyres."

"Roger that..."

By this time the people on board the transports were aware of the conflict going on behind them. The trucks came to a halt and the passengers jumped out onto the road to watch.

"Not what we want them to do," Jack said grimly. "If those blighters manage to launch a rocket it'll be a right bloody mess." The truck picked up speed as it lurched back onto the road and headed for the convoy of would-be voters. "Harry, bring us around and get those tyres, now!"

The frantic chatter of the helicopter's guns followed Jack's bellowed order. The truck below them veered off the road again as its tyres exploded into useless shreds. It came to a grinding halt nose-down in the sand, the man riding in back thrown violently into the air, ending up sprawled face-down on the ground. Three men spilled out of the cab, guns pointed at the helicopter, but they scattered without firing a single shot when Jack and his men opened fire on them, deliberately aiming over their heads, now they had them on the run.

"That should do it, lads," Jack said with satisfaction, shouldering his gun. "We'll ride shotgun for those civilians 'til we reach Dakran. Harry, radio HQ and let them know why we'll be arriving late."

* * * *

Mark woke slowly, conscious only of the pounding headache that started at the back of his skull and pulsed all the way to behind his eyeballs. *Jesus, what the fuck happened?* All he could remember was standing in his tent reading something — oh yeah, a letter from his folks. Then, something, *someone* behind him... Cautiously, he opened his eyes and looked around the dimly lit room. *Where the hell am I?*

"Hello?" His voice was hoarse, the word no more than a croak. His throat was dry, sore. He swallowed, trying to gain a little strength. "Hello?"

A flicker of fear tugged at the pit of his stomach as he sat up and stared around at the unfamiliar surroundings. He'd been abducted, *kidnapped*, and the reasons, although he could only as yet guess at them, filled him with apprehension. If Malouf and his gang had him again, he could bet they would do everything in their power to prevent him escaping a second time. And of course, Jack wouldn't even know he'd been abducted yet again.

Jack...help! He couldn't control the shudder that coursed through him at the thought of what they might be planning for him this time around.

He swung his legs over the side of the bed he was lying on, groaning softly from the pain in his head, barely aware that his only article of clothing was his shorts. He stood unsteadily, peering across the shadowed room, at the shimmering drapes moving gently in the breeze from the open window.

Open... Staggering slightly, he made his way to the window, pushed aside the drapes, then sighed with disappointment. The window might be open, but the iron bars he stared at made escape impossible.

"Ah, you are awake at last, Doctor Hamilton."

The sound of Dhul Fiqar's silken voice made the short hairs on Mark's neck stand up. "I might have known you'd be involved in this, asshole," he snapped, then winced as his head spun from the sudden move he'd made to face Fiqar. "Don't get too close," he managed to gasp. "Remember what happened last time."

"I remember only too well," Fiqar sneered, "but, believe me, you will never have that opportunity again. You are a devious man, Doctor, and for that you will be punished one day."

"Punished?" Despite his pain, Mark barked out a derisive laugh. "By whom, may I ask? Not you, Fiqar. You're too much of a coward to try it alone."

Even in the half-light of the room Fiqar's expression of disdain was plainly visible. "Like all Americans, you are much too arrogant, Doctor. You even considered yourself above Prince Rashid, a member of our country's royalty. To refuse him was very foolish, but he is a patient man."

"Meaning what?"

"Meaning, he is willing to give you a second chance—after you have fallen to your knees and begged for his forgiveness."

"Yeah, well, that's not going to happen," Mark snapped, "so tell the old fossil to forget me, and if he doesn't let me go *pronto*, you guys will be in a shitload of trouble. Kidnapping American citizens is a ser—"
He broke off as two more men, carrying guns, entered the room.

Fiqar sniggered. "The prince guessed that you might be resistant to his offer, but he is willing to wait until you reconsider. You will remain here as his *guest* until then. These gentlemen," he gestured at the two armed men, "will see to it that you do not leave this room—"

"Wait a minute!" Mark started forward, but was brought to a halt by one of the men who pushed the barrel of his gun into Mark's stomach, causing him to choke out, "You son of a bitch, Fiqar. You think you can get away with this?"

"We have already 'got away with this', Doctor Hamilton." Fiqar paused to snicker, then continued in his sneering tone. "You see, no one knows where you are. Your brave friend, Sergeant Major Caruthers, does not even know yet that you are missing from the clinic. I am sure when he finds out, he will be enraged, saddened perhaps, but eventually you will be forgotten."

"Are you nuts?" Mark yelled. "Of course Jack will know where you've taken me. He was here before, remember?"

"Oh, how droll, Doctor. You think you are in the same place? Surely you could give us more credit than that." Fiqar's dark features twisted with derision. "Consider yourself lucky, Doctor. Were I not under instructions to ensure you come to no physical harm, I would take pleasure in punishing you myself. You tricked me once before, inflicted pain upon me. I have not forgotten that, and I promise that when you fall from the prince's favour, I will inflict pain upon you— only it will be a thousand times worse."

"Oh, spare me the fucking dramatics," Mark snarled. "You and the rest of these lunatics are going to be behind bars very soon—"

Fiqar's right hand shot out and he gripped Mark by the jaw, while one of the armed men grabbed Mark's arms. "Be quiet!" Fiqar spat at him. "You are in no position to threaten anyone. You will remain here until you give in to Prince Rashid's wishes. The longer you refuse, the longer you will stay. The choice is yours, Doctor Hamilton. There is no escape, nowhere to hide."

Fiqar squeezed Mark's jaw, a malicious glint in his eyes, and for a moment it seemed the man was going to forget his orders and exact some revenge for the ball crushing he'd suffered, then he slapped Mark's face, hard, and stepped back.

"Asshole," Mark muttered, rubbing his stinging cheek.

"You will be bathed, fed and clothed," Fiqar said, ignoring Mark's insult. "But until your arrogance is replaced with subservience, you will not leave this room." With that, he spun on his heel and left the room, the two guards following. The door was slammed shut and Mark drew in a quick startled breath at the sound of a key being turned.

"Bastards!" he yelled. "You're going to be sorry —" He broke off, realising the futility of raging at a closed and locked door. *"Goddamn it."* How in hell was he going to get out of this mess? Why had he ignored Jack's warnings not to go back to the clinic, and why hadn't he made more of a big deal when DCI didn't even respond to his initial report about the first time he had been kidnapped. He knew they were undermanned and stretched to the limit, but dammit...

Cursing some more under his breath, he found a light switch and flicked it on, then glanced around at his surroundings. The room was richly furnished, too ornate for Mark's taste, but it looked as though he was going to have to get used to it, for a while at least.

Jack was out on a mission, so like Fiqar had said, he wouldn't know of this latest development, maybe even for the next few days, and even if he did find out, he wouldn't be in a position to just quit what he was doing and come look for him. Then again, where would he start? Mark groaned as the possibility of being cooped up in this room for weeks sank in — even worse, if Jack or the authorities never found out where he was being held, he could very well be a prisoner for the rest of his life — or until the aging Prince tired of him. He really didn't want to dwell on the implications of that particular scenario.

He wandered across the room and pushed open a door on the far end. A bathroom — not nearly as opulent as the one in the palace, but beautiful nevertheless. Well, a prisoner he might be, but at least he'd be a clean one.

Chapter Ten

One week later

"Hey, Jack—the Major wants you in his office ASAP!"

Jack stared down at the soldier giving him the message then jumped down from the helicopter he'd just flown back from Dakran in. He nodded his acknowledgement and strode of to the CO's quarters.

This can't be good, he thought. Usually the commanding officer, Major Holbrook, waited for him to come in with his report ready. *Something must be up...* Jack liked the Major, always finding him a fair and intelligent man. He had the feeling he might be gay, even though he'd never seen any indication either in the man's demeanour or through idle gossip. Just a feeling...

He was intercepted by a small figure that ran into his path and grabbed at his hand. "Hey, Ghali." He smiled down at the boy's anxious face. "Why the sad face?"

"Oh, Sergeant Jack..." Ghali's eyes were wide and filled with tears. "The bad men have taken the doctor away."

"*What?*" Jack stopped in his tracks and knelt before the boy. "Where did you hear this?"

"Asima called in yesterday. He has been missing since-"

"Sergeant Major!" Jack tore his eyes from Ghali's stricken expression to see Major Holbrook standing in the doorway of his office. "Come inside please, Jack."

"Yes, sir." He straightened and offered Holbrook a cursory salute. He ruffled Ghali's hair. "Don't worry, young cobber. We'll find him. I'll talk to you later." He followed the major into his office and sat in the chair Holbrook gestured to.

Holbrook stared at him across his desk, the expression on his normally pleasant face grim. "Sergeant Major, I've received a rather disturbing report..."

"Yeah, the kid, Ghali, started to tell me about it," Jack muttered. *Hurry up and get this over with, so I can find out what's happened to Mark...*

Holbrook raised an eyebrow. "Ghali knows nothing about it. No one on base knows yet."

Jack met the Major's stony stare straight on. "He just told me Doctor Hamilton's missing, and —"

"Sergeant — *Jack* — this has nothing to do with Doctor Hamilton's disappearance, regrettable though that is..."

Regrettable? What the hell is this about then?

"You were engaged in a confrontation on the road to Dakran," Holbrook said.

"That's right, sir," Jack replied impatiently. "It's in the report I sent you."

"Your report and" — he lifted a document from his desk — "what I have here, are two very different accounts of what happened."

"I'm not following you."

"Eye witnesses state you attacked and killed two men who were acting as escorts to civilians on their way to Dakran for the election."

Jack snorted in derision. "Bullshit. Those *escorts* were driving a rocket launcher, and gettin' ready to blow the civilians to smithereens. We gave 'em fair warning to stop — it's all in my report, exactly what happened. The other men can vouch for every word."

"I have no doubt they can, and would, Jack, but I can't ignore this complaint. The UN authorities have instructed me to ground you, pending an investigation into the matter —"

"What?" Jack glared at his superior officer. "You believe this muck?"

"That's not what I said, Jack, and you know it, but my hands are tied —"

"What about the doctor?" Jack snapped. "What's been done to find him?"

Holbrook looked surprised by Jack's shift in the conversation. "The doctor? I'm afraid that's not in my jurisdiction — nor yours, Jack," he added, seeing his sergeant's angry expression.

"So, we just forget about him?" Jack demanded.

"The DCI authorities have instigated a search for him, and the security patrol they have in the area is helping."

Jack snorted again. "Those useless arseholes couldn't find a bloody pea in a pod. That bloke they had in charge of 'em was responsible for Mark—the *doctor*—being taken the first time around. He was in cahoots with the slavers, and—"

Holbrook held up a hand to stop Jack's tirade. "Jack, I know all of that. Nevertheless it's outside our jurisdiction, and right now you have more pressing things to worry about. You're going to have to sit down and write a statement regarding this accusation."

"Fuck that," Jack growled. "The doc's a friend of ours. He treated O'Brien's shoulder. Saved him from having a bad infection. He showed he's got balls when it came to dealing with those fuckin' slavers—and now we're just going to leave him to be treated like some…some…fuck—I can't even say it!"

"*Sergeant Major Caruthers*, you have a duty to perform while you're still a member of the Australian Army. Now, take this, read it, and rebut it! That'll be all." Jack lurched to his feet, snapped a salute, then took the document Holbrook handed him. He turned to leave, pausing in the doorway as Holbrook added, "By the way, Jack, it looks like you might have some time on your hands, *after you've taken care of that rebuttal*. Let me know when you might need a vehicle at your disposal."

Jack gaped for a moment at the major. Had he heard him right? Of course he fuckin' had! He saluted again, more smartly this time. "Thank you, Major. I'll get on this…*rebuttal*, straight away."

Ghali was waiting for him outside the Major's office. "You will find the doctor?" he asked, clinging to Jack's hand.

"Yes," Jack replied, and squeezed the boy's hand. "You bet I'll find him." *And when I do*, he thought, *he is never going back to that sodding clinic!*

* * * *

Mark sighed as he awoke to the prospect of yet another mind-numbingly boring day. How many had passed since they'd brought him here? He was beginning to lose track, without a calendar, television, or even a radio to help. And what was it that they expected of him—that this boredom would drive him into the arms of an octogenarian for a session of spank the monkey?

No way. No *fucking* way... Not even if they kept him holed up here for the next millennium. At least by then the old pervert wouldn't want him. *I'll be old and grizzled too.* The thought made him chuckle despite himself. Too bad he wouldn't have Jack to grow old and grizzled with.

"Where are you, Jack?" he said aloud, staring up at the ceiling. "Have you found out yet that I'm missing, presumed—?" Well, God knows what they've presumed. Thinking of Jack and their time together always made him hard, and this morning was no exception. He'd jerked off several times when the memories of the way Jack had fucked him swam in his mind. So hungry and forceful, then afterwards so sweet and tender. He could remember every detail of the last time they'd made love. Made love... Yes, now in Mark's mind what they'd shared was so much more than mere sex. He remembered Jack's kisses, always so sweetly sensual before the hungry passion took over. He slid a hand over his chest, teasing a nipple between his fingers, imagining Jack's lips nuzzling at the small peak of flesh, of it hardening under his touch. Mark writhed at the thought, his hand moving down to grasp his burgeoning erection, his lips parting at the memory of Jack's mouth on his —

His hand leapt away from his hardening cock when the door was flung open and Omar, along with an armed guard, entered the room. Either Omar or Hassan, the two brothers who had 'attended' him at the prince's palace, brought Mark's meals each day, always punctual and always with a sweet smile of deference. Mark had a suspicion that beneath the sweetness lurked a certain viciousness he might yet see manifest itself, if he didn't start to cooperate. But not today... Mark had discovered both brothers spoke a fair amount of English, although they rarely did, unless Mark insisted when his Arabic gave out.

"*Effendi,*" Omar murmured, placing a tray of fruit, a glass of orange juice and a cup of strong black coffee on the table near Mark's bed.

"Thanks, Omar." Mark formed his lips into the semblance of a smile as he stared up into the Arab boy's dark eyes. He saw a slight hesitation in the boy's movements, a faint tremble in his hands when he stepped back from Mark's bed. *Yeah, I know you want in my pants, Omar, but that ain't gonna happen, and your life would be worth nothing if old Rashid ever caught on to what's going through your mind right now...*

Omar bowed slightly, then turned away, leaving the room accompanied by the armed guard. Despite the fact he expected it, the sound of the door being locked made Mark groan and fall back on his bed. Just how much longer could he stand this? It didn't look like anyone was coming to his rescue, so the best thing he could do was work on some way to escape by himself. But how? And just where in hell was he anyway?

He had a vague recollection of engine noise at some point after he'd been rendered unconscious, but that could have been any vehicle used to transport him — even a plane? He shuddered as he considered the idea he might have been flown out of the country and into some province where the prince had another hideaway. From the window he could see only palm trees and lush vegetation, but he had an inkling that somewhere there was an unseen high wall screening the place from the outside world. Prince Rashid might be affiliated with Saudi royalty, but what he did would be frowned on by his family and peers, hence the reason for secrecy.

As he sipped his orange juice he wondered what would happen to the likes of Omar and Hassan when the old fossil kicked the bucket. He found it hard to believe that Rashid would actually provide for his entourage after his demise. Then again, the old guy might be genuinely fond of the boys — fond enough not to see any harm come to them.

Hmm...if he could just overpower the guard and hold either Omar or Hassan hostage, using them as barter for his release. But overpowering the hulking monolith that followed the boys each time they entered the room would take some doing. The guy was a good five inches taller than Mark, and easily outweighed him by fifty or even sixty pounds. Maybe he could stand behind the door and brain him as he passed through. He was pretty sure he could restrain either one of the boys — but what if Rashid didn't give a flying fuck about them and instructed the other guards to shoot Omar or Hassan, just to get them out of the way? As much as he wanted to get of his prison he couldn't, in all conscience, put the boys in that kind of danger—even though they were a part of the problem.

Damn... He picked up a piece of mango and slipped it into his mouth, sucking on the juice thoughtfully. Of course, there was always the chance that the guys at Care International had instigated a search for him. Maybe they, and eventually *he*, might get lucky...maybe.

* * * *

"So what do they think happened to the doc?" Paddy asked as he watched Jack stow equipment and provisions into the Jeep he was borrowing 'for a few days'.

"*They* don't know," Jack replied bitterly, "but I'll bet you fifty quid it was those fuckin' slavers again. They were pissed he slipped through their fingers, and it cost that Malouf character a dollar or two, without a doubt." He didn't add that the fact Malouf had been stiffed because of Jack's arrival, guns blazing and breaking up the deal, had filled him with a whole lot of satisfaction at the time. Now though... Maybe he should have been a helluva lot more insistent that Mark didn't return to the clinic. Trouble was, Mark had thought Jack was acting like too much of a heavy in any case, so no matter what he'd have said, Mark would have ignored him, and done what he wanted to do. *Fuckin' stubborn Yank...*

"Where are you going to start looking?"

Jack sighed. "That's the rub, as they say, Paddy. I don't have a fuckin' clue where they might have taken him, but I have a bloody good idea that security bloke Fiqar does."

Jack had contacted the security headquarters Fiqar reported to and had been informed that Fiqar was AWOL. The rather chatty young security officer Jack got a hold of told him that Fiqar's brother, who also worked for the security company, had been questioned by his superior officers, and after some hedging, had admitted Fiqar had spent a night at his mother's home just outside Khartoum. Apparently, he was waiting to hear from some 'business associates'.

"He'll be a lot easier to find," Jack continued, "and when I do, I'll squeeze him 'til he tells me — or his eyes pop out of his head, whichever comes first."

Paddy chuckled. "Good luck then, Sarge. Wish I could come with you, but the Major says you're on your own for this one."

"Yeah...but thanks for the offer, Paddy. I told the Major I'd keep in touch, unofficially of course."

He beckoned Ghali over. The little boy had been hovering behind Paddy, his eyes wide with apprehension. "Sergeant Jack, I would come with you to find the doctor," he whispered, looking up at Jack with a wistful expression.

Jack smiled but shook his head. "You're better off here, Ghali. I don't want you anywhere near the characters I'll be meeting up with." He crouched down and gave the boy a hug. "Don't worry, I'll bring Doc back, safe and sound." Ghali clung to him, his slender body trembling, his tears wetting Jack's neck. "Come on now," Jack crooned in the boy's ear. "It'll all be hunky-dory, just you wait and see. We'll be back before you know it."

Ghali pulled back a little, his tear-filled eyes meeting Jack's in a doubtful gaze. "I would pray to Allah for you," he said on a choking sob, "but He didn't listen to me when I asked Him not to let my father give me away."

Jack felt an ache in his chest as he held the boy in a close hug. "Pray anyway, Ghali," he whispered. "I think I'll need all the help I can get."

Chapter Eleven

Khartoum

The city of Khartoum was approximately a four hour drive across rough territory from Jack's base. He had no illusions that when he got there, everyone would be eager to tell him where Fiqar was, and how he could find Mark. All he could hope for was a lead – if he could find Fiqar or Malouf, he'd at least be on the right track. Prince Rashid obviously had a lot of influence, and a lot of money, but even he couldn't keep moving around forever. And it was unlikely he'd get any help from his Saudi relations. Rashid must have built his own private world with his own funds, and Jack was pretty certain the men who worked for him did it for monetary gain, rather than any deep-seated loyalty.

Jack's main fear was that the prince might tire of the game he was playing with Mark, dispose of him in such a way he would never be found, without involvement traceable back to Rashid. He knew he was fighting against time. Mark would not give in easily, perhaps not at all, and the prince would eventually resort to punishment in order to break the doctor's spirit. Jack seethed, and at the same time shuddered at the thought of Mark's smooth skin being flayed from his body by some vicious whipping. If that happened, whoever was responsible would pay — big time!

Khartoum teemed with life as Jack drove through the centre of town, passing the huge open market place jammed to capacity with traders and customers alike clamouring for service and attention. The address he'd been given for Fiqar's mother's home was in a well established area, just outside and to the north the city limits, across the Kober Bridge. The heat was crushing, well over a hundred degrees Fahrenheit, and Jack found himself looking forward to the darkness when the temperatures would fall to a more acceptable cooler degree.

The GPS system on the Jeep's dash indicated he was about a hundred yards or so from his destination. He wasn't expecting a warm reception at the home of Fiqar's mother. Most likely she'd be hostile and uncooperative, but it was the only lead he had so far — and just maybe she wasn't too fond of the kind of company her son was keeping these days.

Jack slowed the Jeep as two men stepped into the road ahead of him, both carrying guns. *Well…shit…looks like I'm expected, but how the hell…?*

The men waved him down, guns levelled at the Jeep. "*Salam wa aleikum,*" Jack greeted the men, pasting a smile on his face like he was auditioning for a toothpaste ad. His greeting was not returned. One man hopped aboard the Jeep, keeping his gun trained on Jack's chest, while the other waved him into an almost hidden driveway. Ahead, Jack could see a one-story house painted a dazzling white, surrounded by tall palm trees and lush vegetation.

"Out," growled the man holding his weapon on Jack. Seeing no point in arguing, and figuring these guys were somehow connected to his search for Mark, Jack shrugged then slid his tall frame out of the Jeep. The man shouldered Jack's gun, then jumped from the Jeep while the other signalled for Jack to spread them. The handgun and knife he'd secreted were quickly found and stuck into the man's belt, then he was pushed towards the house.

So Fiqar's mother has her own private army, Jack thought wryly as he was shoved and steered to an open doorway. His eyes narrowed in recognition as a familiar looking figure appeared in the open door.

"*Malouf*...should've known you'd show your ugly mug sooner or later."

The Turkish slave trader's smile was anything but pleasant. "Sergeant Major Caruthers, we've been expecting you."

"Really? Just how the hell did you manage that?"

Malouf's muddy brown eyes gleamed with a nasty light. "It was obvious to us that when you discovered the fair doctor was missing, you would attempt a rescue mission. Naturally, we could not allow that, so we forwarded the erroneous information that this house belonged to Dhul Fiqar's mother, knowing you would immediately follow up on that lead."

"So, you got me — what now?"

"You will be disposed of, of course — after I have exacted a little revenge for the loss of my men and the humiliation you caused me in front of His Highness, Prince Rashid."

Jack snorted. "You're nothing if not bloody predictable. Just tell me this—where is Doctor Hamilton? Is he here?"

"That knowledge will not help you, Sergeant Major, but no, he is not here. He is in another of the prince's lavish palaces, enjoying the prince's hospitality." Malouf's thick lips parted in a sly smile. "No doubt he will soon succumb to the luxury of the life he is being offered."

"I truly doubt that," Jack snarled.

Malouf feigned surprise. "But why do you say that? What man does not long for riches and a life of ease?"

"A man with principles, like Doctor Hamilton—but you wouldn't know anything about that, would you, you fuckin' wanker."

Malouf growled and backhanded Jack across the face. "That's right, make me hate you all the more, so that your screams of pain will sound sweet on my ears." He gestured impatiently at his two lackeys. "Take him inside."

* * * *

Mark bit his lip as under the watchful eye of the armed guard, Omar and Hassan stripped him of the clothing he'd been provided, and prepared him for his first meeting with Prince Rashid. He'd resisted at first, trying to make it clear he could undress and dress by himself, but after the guard had swung his Uzi in Mark's direction and a stream of excited words had bubbled out of Omar's mouth, only a few of which he understood, he'd given in. He'd got the gist, however, and couldn't quite dispel the feeling of nausea that roiled in his stomach.

He would be presented to the prince, who had grown impatient and would wait no longer. Mark wondered what the option would be. No way was he going to give in to the old man's advances, and when he refused again, he figured he would either be forced at gunpoint to do whatever the prince wished – or shot. Mark shuddered. Not much of an option.

He sighed as Omar fussed with his hair, trying to comb the unruly blond curls into some semblance of order. Maybe if he'd shaved it all off, it would have been enough of a turn off for the prince to change his mind about keeping him as a sex toy. He shuddered again – *sex toy. Jesus, Jack...* He thought of how he'd joked about being Jack's fuck toy and how quickly Jack had turned so sweetly serious, telling Mark he was much more than that to him...

Oh, hell... Mark's eyes glistened as he brought back the memory of being in Jack's arms, the way they had given themselves up to the hungry passion that enveloped them every time they were alone together. His thoughts were abruptly interrupted by Hassan tugging on his sleeve.

"*Ta'ala ma'ee,*" the boy muttered, and Mark nodded, following him from the room.

Mark looked around as they walked down the lengthy hallway. This was the first time he'd been out of the room he'd been confined to since his abduction. Again, the place reeked of money – marble walls and floors, scattered rugs and wall hangings, vases and sculptures of all shapes and sizes – and this was just a hallway! Mark shook his head at the extravagance surrounding him, and wondered what lay ahead.

He didn't have long to wonder, for when they entered a large room at the end of the hall, he spotted Rashid sitting on an ornate chair, seemingly asleep. Mark couldn't resist the wry thought that the old guy didn't seem *that* excited at the prospect of seeing the man he'd gone to so much trouble to bring here. Rashid raised his head slowly and fixed a dull stare on Mark. He muttered something unintelligible and Mark was pushed nearer to him.

He's sick, Mark thought with interest, noticing the sweat dampening Rashid's brow. Was *this* the reason he'd been brought here? Not as a sex toy at all, but as a *doctor? Wait, that's not rational. Rashid must have access to a hundred doctors if he wanted one…*

"*Ana mareed*,' the prince mumbled. "I am sick." He followed the weakly spoken statement with a series of hacking coughs.

Mark nodded. "Yes, I can see that." *Pneumonia most likely*, he thought. "What can I do for you?"

"You are a doctor, yes?"

"I am—but I would've thought you had your own personal physician."

"He has been forbidden to attend me," the prince said, his breath catching in his throat. "My family has decided it is time for me to die. They are ashamed of me, you see, and therefore of no consequence. Make me well, Doctor, and I will see you are well rewarded."

"And you'll let me go, afterwards?"

The prince smiled thinly, then nodded. "You are a very beautiful young man, Doctor, but in my present condition I am hardly able to appreciate you. To attend me in my sickness was not the reason I had you brought here, but Allah has seen fit to give you both beauty and a talent for healing — so yes, heal me and I shall let you return home."

Without asking permission, Mark took the prince's wrist in a gentle grip to feel his pulse. "I don't have any of my supplies here."

"We will get you what you need."

Mark had no doubt that despite his family's disapproval, Rashid still held a significant influence in the area. "I'll prepare a list," he said. "In the meantime, you should be in bed. You have a fever, and you are severely dehydrated. Do you have a supply of bottled water?" Weakly, the prince nodded. Mark beckoned Omar and Hassan over. "Take the prince to his bedroom and make sure he rests until the supplies I need are here — and make sure he drinks plenty of water."

Well, he thought as he watched the boys support the prince and walk him slowly from the room, *here's a switch I hadn't seen coming. I just hope the old guy is as good as his word. Yeah, Jack, maybe we'll be getting together sooner than we expected!*

* * * *

Jack stood in the centre of the small empty room he'd been pushed into and took stock of his surroundings. Okay, there was a window, high enough to be just out of reach. There was nothing to stand on to enable him to even reach the sill, and he figured the window was too small to allow him to squeeze through anyway.

Damn... So far, Malouf's threat of exquisite torture hadn't been carried out. They'd roughed him up some, but nothing too serious, and he'd managed to get a couple of punches in, making them realise they'd better wait until the rest of Malouf's gang arrived. Safety in numbers, he supposed with a wry grin. If he could just get that one guard on the other side of the door... He turned as he heard the sound of voices outside the door. *Oh, oh...maybe the gang's all here.*

The door swung open and Malouf along with Fiqar entered.

"Well, well, wondered when you'd show up." Jack smirked at Fiqar. "Balls back to normal are they?"

Fiqar flushed under his swarthy skin while Malouf sniggered. "You will soon be screaming to have your balls returned to you, Sergeant Major... Or perhaps we will save them for your doctor lover," he added snidely.

"The doctor will be far too busy pleasuring Prince Rashid to wonder how you are faring." Fiqar's eyes glittered as he sneered at Jack. "How does that make you feel?" he asked, his eyes gleaming with malice. "To know the man you want is now servicing another for money? That the promise of wealth will allow even an old and withered man like Rashid to slobber over him. Does that make you angry, infidel?"

"Bloody hell," Jack said, laughing. "Who writes your dialogue, mate? You sound like you're in some grade-B flick I saw when I was a nipper. All you have to do is twirl your moustache—if you could grow one, arsehole."

Fiqar stepped forward, arm raised to strike Jack, his arrogance blinding him to danger. Mistake. Jack's hand shot out, grabbing Fiqar's wrist in a vice-like grip making the man squeal with pain. Jack then pulled Fiqar to him, encircling the man's throat with his own arm in a Japanese stranglehold while digging his clenched fist into the area over Fiqar's kidney.

Malouf, his eyes wide with shock, screamed for his men, and three of the thugs piled into the room. "Shoot him," Malouf yelled.

"I can't get a clean shot," one of the men muttered, trying to aim past Fiqar.

"Never mind Fiqar," Malouf spat. "Shoot!"

"Nice friends you got," Jack hissed in Fiqar's ear, as the man squeaked with fear. He jerked Fiqar off his feet, and threw him at the gunmen. Four bodies crashed to the floor in a tangle of arms and legs, guns clattering all around. Malouf shrieked with rage and pulled his own gun only to have it violently knocked from his hand by a kick from Jack's big right foot, then his jaw almost broken by a punch from Jack's fist that laid the slave trader out, unconscious.

Jack kicked the slavers' guns out of reach into the passageway outside the room. He grabbed Fiqar by the shirt collar, dragged him to his feet, then threw him through the door. He delivered a couple of punches at two of the men who tried to get up, before following Fiqar through the door.

"Lock it," he ordered tersely, picking up two guns and levelling one at Fiqar. Shaking, Fiqar did as he was told, then his head jerked up as two more men charged down the passageway towards them.

"Help! Shoot him!" Fiqar screamed.

Jack didn't hesitate. He swung both guns in the men's direction and sent two sharp bursts of lethal fire, cutting the men down in mid-stride.

"Outside," Jack snarled at Fiqar, smacking him hard with the muzzle of one gun. The ex-security officer yelped and stumbled forward as Jack pushed him towards the exit. His Jeep was still there, and he noticed with satisfaction the keys were still in the ignition.

"Okay…" He flattened Fiqar against a wall, one arm pressed up against Fiqar's throat. "Where'd they take him?"

"I don't know."

Jack lifted his knee and shoved it into Fiqar's crotch. "One more time—where'd they take him, Fuckar… You get only one more chance then I crush your already swollen balls, for good."

Fiqar wriggled in fear. Jack pressed his knee in harder. Fiqar squeaked. Jack rammed his knee further into the man's balls. Fiqar sagged against the wall and gasped, "All right, all right, I'll tell you. The prince has a retreat in Eritrea, on the coast near Bahri. They took him there to—"

"I know why they took him there, arsehole," Jack said through gritted teeth. "Have they hurt him?"

Fiqar shook his head. "No, no. I was there two days ago and he was still…untouched."

"And he better stay that way, or you're a dead man."

"The prince wants him acquiescent," Fiqar gasped, rubbing his throat. "Everyone has been ordered not to harm him."

"Well, they're gonna have a long wait for the doc to agree to anything that old geezer has in mind"

Jack stepped back and Fiqar slumped down. "Draw me a map, and make sure it's accurate, or I find you again, and make sure you don't get to breed anymore little Fuckars like you."

Jack marched him back indoors and sat him at a table, training his gun on him until the man had finished drawing a map of the location in Eritrea where Rashid had his 'retreat'. Then before Fiqar could protest, Jack found a length of rope and secured him to the chair.

"Someday, someone may come by to check out the noise coming from here," Jack said with a final pull on the rope. "'Til then, g'day."

Chapter Twelve

Mark stared down at the old man lying on the huge, opulent bed. The bed's size made Rashid look tinier and more wizened than ever. He gazed back at Mark through red rimmed, pain filled eyes, and for the first time, Mark actually felt sorry for the man who had abducted him.

The drugs he had ordered had arrived, and he had already administered the azithromycin pills he hoped would kill the bacteria and reduce the inflammation in Rashid's lungs. He managed a small smile as he leant over the prince, warming the cool metal of his stethoscope with the palm of his hand, before placing it on the old man's chest. He listened to the stentorian breathing for a few moments, knowing it would be some time before he knew if the drug would have any good effect.

"Will I live, Doctor?" Rashid wheezed.

"You should really be in hospital," Mark replied.

"Impossible, but you can have anything you need to facilitate my healing."

Mark nodded. That much was true. Expense was no object, obviously. Everything he'd asked for, the antibiotics, stethoscope, and the oxygen tanks had been purchased, although he was curious as to how they had procured the antibiotics. In the States, such things could only be acquired through prescription, but then, this wasn't the States, and his patient, although ostracized by his family, must surely have some influence, along with lots of money.

Omar and his brother, Hassan, hovered around the bed, looks of concern on their boyish faces. Once again, Mark wondered just what would happen to them if Rashid kicked the bucket. Was it the prince's poor health that caused them to worry, or the uncertainty of their future should he pop it? One thing Mark was almost certain of, Rashid's family would not look after these guys.

"Well, all we can do now is wait to see if your system responds to the antibiotics," Mark said quietly. "Make sure you continue to drink plenty water or fruit juice. Have Omar or Hassan stay with you. I will check on you in a few hours." He paused then asked, "Am I free to walk in the grounds? I've had no fresh air in several days."

Rashid closed his eyes but told Hassan the doctor should be allowed to stroll in the grounds. A sinister chuckle escaped the prince's lips as he added that the walls were high enough to prevent escape.

Mark had expected that. Better than nothing, he supposed. "Thanks," he muttered, then followed Hassan from Rashid's bedroom.

The air outside smelt sweet and fresh, and despite his serious predicament, Mark found pleasure in walking through the lushly landscaped grounds. He couldn't help wondering just where in the world he was. Definitely not the desert. He could smell the ocean on the breeze that cooled his face.

"Hey, Hassan...just where are we, in relation to uh...say, Khartoum?"

Hassan didn't reply. *Could it be he actually doesn't know, or has he been instructed not to tell me anything?* Mark shrugged his shoulders and turned away, continuing his walk. As he strolled by some ornamental fountains, he paused to put a hand under the trickling water. He wondered just how the prince would go about releasing him once he'd recovered. He couldn't just shove him through the gates and say, 'Bon voyage,' or its equivalent in Arabic. Or could he?

'Yes, you are free to go, Doctor Hamilton. Thanks for curing me – now, if you won't put out, beat it – oh, and by the way, the US is that-a-way!' He smiled wryly at his thoughts, and stopped to sit on a bench under a huge banyan tree, while Hassan and the guard watched him from a distance of several feet.

Haven't seen this one before...nice looking guy, Mark thought, taking in the guard's slim build and fine featured face. *How'd he get mixed up with this bunch of reprobates?* But then, he hadn't failed to notice that almost all of Rashid's 'employees' were young and easy on the eye. Were they all gay? he wondered, and did they all have to service the prince? He found it hard to imagine the old guy had that much sexual stamina. Maybe he just liked eye candy...

"*Salam,*" he said, smiling at the guard. "*Mā ismak?*" The young guard shook his head and did not reply.

"Jeez, I just want to know your name." He pointed to himself. "*Esmee* Mark." He received a stony stare from dark eyes for his efforts. Mark shrugged and stood up, continuing his walk. He stopped after crossing a small bridge over a koi pond, dropped face down on the ground and started doing push ups. He'd been exercising in his room since his captivity, but it felt great to be doing it outdoors, and if he could prolong his time outside, he would. After about fifty he bounded to his feet and turned to grin at the guard, but found no sign of him, or Hassan.

Funny, where'd they go?

He walked back over the bridge, peering into the dense bushes on either side of the pathway. Then he saw them. Hassan was on his knees in front of the guard and had the man's cock in his mouth, giving him what looked to Mark like a very skilful blow job. The young guard's eyes were closed, his head dropped back in apparent ecstasy, while his fingers caressed Hassan's face and curly hair. Hassan was gazing up at him with loving eyes. Mark was transfixed by what he saw, and he could feel his own arousal growing inside his shorts. He knew he should just walk away and wait somewhere for them to finish, but found he was unable to tear himself away from the intensely erotic scene.

Hassan pulled the guard's pants down around his hips, and palmed the curvature of his buttocks. Mark watched, his mouth slightly open, as Hassan's fingers probed between the guard's plump butt cheeks. The man's hips bucked, he let out a gasping groan as Hassan pulled him forward, then his whole body shuddered as he climaxed, his cock trapped inside Hassan's eager mouth.

Wow... Mark stepped back and made his way onto the path as quietly as he could. So that was the way of it—Hassan and the young guard doing stuff that old Rashid wouldn't approve of in a month of Sundays. He wondered how they'd managed to hook up in the first place. It had been quite obvious this wasn't their first time alone together. It had been far too intimate for a first encounter.

He grinned at the two men as they appeared on the pathway. "Hey, don't let me get in the way." He winked at Hassan. "Enjoy. I'm happy to sit here and wait."

Hassan placed one hand on his companion's arm and said something in a low voice Mark couldn't catch. The guard threw Mark a wary look, then scowled at Hassan. There wasn't an inkling of a friendly smile on his face as he approached Mark, just a slight upward movement of his gun, indicating he should move on back to the house. He sighed. Oh well, he'd tried to be friendly, show he understood their situation. Maybe in a few days, once old Rashid improved, he'd be getting the hell out of here anyway.

* * * *

Jack stood on the side of the road glaring at the Jeep. He kicked one of the tyres in an impotent rage. *Fuckin' piece of shit!* First, one of Malouf's bastards had lifted the GPS system out of the Jeep—*bloody thieving wanker*—and Jack hadn't noticed until he was on the other side of Khartoum that the damned thing was missing. He'd been cursing the fact he only had Fiqar's roughly drawn map to follow, and that didn't show anything outside of the coastal region of Eritrea.

Now this... He'd had a bad feeling the Jeep wasn't going to manage the trek across the desert. Just as well it hadn't broken down half way there, stuck in the middle of nowhere. Nothing else for it...he'd have to go back to Khartoum, if he could find a friendly soul to take him that far, and get some help from the UN officials there. He'd just have to think of some bloody good reasons why they should...

At the UN agency, a young man with cool Norwegian good looks and an icy expression to match, stared up at Jack as though he were mad. "You want *what?*" he asked, his arched eyebrows almost reaching his hairline.

Jack considered his gaydar infallible, so he'd targeted the young Norwegian as the most likely to be won over. He glanced at the man's name tag. "I want to borrow a Jeep in good nick, Eirik, or better still a chopper with a reliable pilot."

"And who *are* you, exactly?"

"Sergeant Major Jack Caruthers, Australian Army Special Ops., attached to the UN peacekeeping force, here in the Sudan—'bout hundred miles from Khartoum. I want to get to Eritrea where some rascal of a prince named Rashid is holding a friend of mine against his will. He's a doctor with Doctors Who Care International, y'see, and he was kidnapped about a week ago, and not yet been found. I have a lead as to his whereabouts, but the ruddy Jeep I was driving is about to give up on me, so I need transportation to get on my way, ASAP."

Eirik continued to stare at Jack as though mesmerised, his cold expression rapidly thawing. Jack wasn't a conceited man but he could tell the young

Norwegian fancied him. That, after all, was what he'd bargained for.

"And this doctor," Eirik finally said, "isn't DCI trying to find him?"

Jack nodded. "They've been trying, but so far they've had no luck."

"His name?"

"Mark Hamilton. Doctor Mark Hamilton."

Eirik punched some keys on his computer. " Ah, yes...missing for several days... But you mentioned you have a lead. Shouldn't you pass that on to them?"

"Well, you see my problem with that is they'll probably want to negotiate with the bastards who have Mark, uh, Doctor Hamilton, and there's no way they'll ever own up to holding him, so then the DCI blokes will go away, shrugging their shoulders, and saying something about wrong information, and meanwhile the doc will be a goner—" Jack slammed his fist down on Eirik's desk. "And I'll be pissed as hell!"

Eirik rolled his chair back in alarm at Jack's sudden flash of anger. "*Sergeant Major, please...*"

Jack was contrite. "Sorry, Eirik, didn't mean to blow up like that at you. I know you'll give me a helping hand. See, the doctor and me, well, we're very close, if you catch my drift..."

Eirik nodded. He caught Jack's drift very well indeed, and was momentarily caught up in a fantasy where he had a boyfriend who looked like Jack, and who would set out to rescue him from dangerous kidnappers. Eirik's cock jumped inside his boxer shorts at the thought.

"You do realise," he said, his voice decidedly husky, "that in order to requisition a vehicle for you, there is a mountain of paperwork involved."

Jack groaned. "Eirik, I don't have time for red tape. I've already lost a day and a half. If I don't find Mark...the doctor...soon, it might be too late. God knows what they might have done to him..."

"Why did they kidnap him?"

"They're slavers—need I say more?"

Eirik blanched. "My God...you must find him!"

"Right, so how 'bout that vehicle?"

The young Norwegian held out a key ring. "My Hummer is parked out back. It's black with my name on the plate. Just please bring it back when you have found him, okay?"

Jack beamed at him. "You got it, Eirik. I could kiss you right now."

Eirik beamed back at him with anticipation. His lower lip visibly trembled, then he quickly cleared his throat and looked nervously around the office.

Jack chuckled. "Well, later, maybe. Oh, one more thing—I need a map!"

* * * *

On his way back to his room, Mark looked in on his patient, Hassan and the unsmiling guard at his heels. "How is he?" he asked Omar, who sat by Rashid's bed, reading a book.

He looked up at Mark. "He sleeps..."

"Good." Mark felt the old man's pulse. It was steadier than before, and his breathing seemed easier. Rashid was obviously stronger than he looked. "He'll be fine in a couple of days," he told Omar, who surprised him with a look of sadness. *Thought that might cheer you up.*

"Doctor..." It appeared Omar was about to say something, then apparently thought better of it. Instead, he looked across the room at his brother, a question in his eyes. Mark turned to stare at Hassan who once again had his hand on the young guard's arm.

What the heck is going on? The tension in the room was almost palpable. "What's wrong?" he asked Hassan.

No-name muttered something under his breath to Hassan who nodded. "Nothing is wrong, Doctor. My brother is concerned about His Highness's condition, that is all."

"Oh, well, like I said, he's going to be all right." Mark shrugged. "So..." He addressed the guard. "Mr. Laugh-a-minute, I guess you'd better take me back to my room — unless you feel like giving me the run of the place."

As usual, Mark's attempt at humour was lost on the handsome young guard. Stepping away from Hassan he waved his gun at Mark, signalling he should leave. Mark sighed and walked towards the door, again with Hassan and the guard behind him.

When they reached Mark's room, Hassan said, "I will bring your dinner in a few minutes, *effendi.*" Then he closed the door and locked it.

Mark stood by the door listening to the murmur of voices on the other side, one, Hassan, quietly insistent, the other slightly gloomy. His eyes narrowed with interest when he heard Hassan say, "*Uhibbok, uhibbok As'ad...* I love you, I love you, As'ad..."

So the guard had a name—As'ad—and it looked like he and Hassan shared a love that no doubt old Rashid would not be particularly happy about. The voices fell silent and Mark guessed Hassan had gone to fetch his dinner from the kitchen, leaving As'ad on duty outside the door.

Mark figured Hassan and As'ad wouldn't be the only two members of Rashid's staff to have some kind of relationship. Most of the men Rashid 'employed' were young and hot, so connections had to be inevitable—but Mark wondered what the outcome of such a connection might be. The fact that As'ad didn't seem too keen to express any affection towards Hassan in front of him, spoke volumes. Well, he shouldn't feel too sorry for them—they were quite willing to see him kept as a prisoner at the prince's whim, until Rashid's illness made Mark more valuable as a doctor than a sex toy. Still, he couldn't help hoping the guys might find a happy ending. In Mark's opinion, As'ad definitely needed someone in his life to lighten him up a bit.

When Hassan returned about half an hour later with Mark's dinner, a lamb stew over rice which smelled delicious, Mark noticed the young man kept his eyes averted from his.

"Hey, Hassan..." Mark looked over Hassan's shoulder at As'ad as he said, "If you two ever need somewhere to make out, you can use this room. I'll go sit in the bathroom—"

"Doctor!" Hassan stared at him with shock. "Such a thing would have As'ad banished from the prince's service."

"Is that such a bad thing?" Mark asked. "Are you telling me you guys actually *like* being here? Cooped up in this place without a life on the outside? Waiting hand and foot on a man who uses you and others for his pleasure?"

"*Effendi, please...*" Hassan backed away from him, his eyes roaming upwards. "Eyes and ears are everywhere..." Hastily he turned and almost ran from the room, followed quickly by a puzzled As'ad.

"Oh, *shit...*" Mark tried not to look up at the spot between wall and ceiling that Hassan had inadvertently exposed while trying to warn him not to say anymore. The room was bugged. He should have thought of that. Most likely whoever controlled the TV monitors had been watching him night and day, either reporting his movements back to Rashid, or the old guy himself got his jollies by ogling him via TV as he walked about the room naked, or jerked off — thinking of Jack. Mark felt his face grow hot with embarrassment and anger. Those *bastards...* Who knew how many had been watching him every day since he'd been held there. Maybe before Rashid let him go he'd give him a piece of his mind. *Somebody should tell the old fuck he's a piece of shit!*

His appetite gone, he pushed away the tray of food Hassan had brought him and lay down on his bed. All he could do now was hope Rashid would show signs of recovery by the morning, and he'd be one step closer to being released from this stinking place!

* * * *

He awoke to the sound of voices outside his room. Glancing at his watch he could see it was one-twenty in the morning. Who the hell was making a racket at this time of the morning? *Sounds like an argument*, he thought, rolling off the bed and making his way to the door so he could hear better. It was an argument and from the sounds of it, it was Omar and Hassan. *What the heck can they be doing outside my room at this hour?*

"Hey, you guys, what's going on?" he yelled. He stepped back as the door swung open and a frightened looking Omar entered the room.

"You must come with us, Doctor," Omar said, his voice trembling with fear. "Quickly, before the guards know what we are about."

"What do you mean?" Mark stared at the young man, then over his shoulder at Hassan and As'ad who looked really pissed. "The prince has promised I'll be released once he's better."

Omar gave his head a vehement shake. "No, he will not release you. His promises mean nothing. My brother and I were to be here for only one year then sent back to our family with a handsome reward. That was two years ago. We are prisoners here just like you. But we have planned our escape and with the help of As'ad we go tonight."

Mark looked thoughtfully at Omar's brother. "Let me guess — you're not crazy about taking me along."

"Omar endangers our plan by including you," Hassan agreed without any apology in his voice. "But he is right. His Highness will not release you when he is recovered. He has told us he will make you submit to his will, no matter what it takes."

"That son of a bitch," Mark hissed. "So, what's the plan?"

"We go tonight." Hassan displayed more than a hint of impatience. "Before Prince Rashid is able to hear and see the video of what you said earlier. I have disabled the cameras, but it will not be long before they are repaired, and when they are, they will see me acting suspiciously. I will be questioned, punished, and forbidden to attend you again. Omar will also fall under suspicion because he is my brother. We are leaving tonight. You may come with us or stay — your decision."

"Okay, but how do you plan on getting out of here? You've got As'ad, but there's gotta be at least five or six other guards around. Did you bribe them or something?"

"There are only two on patrol right now." Omar sounded confident. "The others are asleep, as is His Highness. He does not know we are not in his room watching over him, and As'ad offered to take over the shift of guarding your room."

"We have access to any number of vehicles," Hassan interrupted. "I have the keys here," he added, dangling a set in front of Mark, "to a powerful Mercedes the prince particularly likes."

Hmm... Mark could hear the smugness in Hassan's voice. *Sounds like he's enjoying giving old Rashid the shaft...* "But what about when he finds you've gone? Won't he send his men after you?"

"We have taken care of that," Hassan said, again with the smugness.

"Okay." Mark started pulling his clothes on. "Ready when you are."

* * * *

Jack parked the Hummer on a ridge overlooking the sprawling walled estate that, as far as he could tell, covered at least a couple of acres of prime coastline. The full moon illuminated the entire estate, and Jack could see very clearly through his binoculars, that the place looked unguarded.

Strange... He would have bet a month's wages Rashid would've had the place crawling with guards. He cocked his head and looked up into the clear night sky at the sound of a helicopter engine approaching from the east. Training his binoculars on the craft he tried to make out the markings on the side, but they didn't look familiar. He focussed on the estate again, his breath escaping in a hiss of surprise as he caught sight of a small group of men running from the house and climbing into a large black car.

"What the...?" One of the men looked familiar. He sharpened the focus on the binoculars. *Very* familiar. "Doc...what the hell?" he muttered. "Where are you going?" From what he could see, it didn't look like Mark was being forced to get in the car. One guy was in fatigues though...security maybe. Whatever, he didn't like the look of this at all. If Mark wasn't being taken under duress, the only alternative could be he was part of an escape plan. A plan, that unless Jack was mistaken, was about to come to a rapid end, for as the car sped through the open gates, the helicopter he'd spotted earlier suddenly dropped from the sky, hovered in front of the car, preventing it from going anywhere. The car reversed, then tried to go around the chopper, but a burst of gunfire sent the vehicle careening off the road. It came to a jarring stop, nose down in a gully.

"Jesus H. Christ!" Jack dove into the Hummer, then with a screech of tyres, tore down the rutted hillside road towards the car.

Chapter Thirteen

Mark, the only one who had secured his seat belt, was dazed but conscious and able to focus on the others in the car. Omar, who'd been sitting next to him, had been rammed headfirst into the back of the driver seat. Mark leant over and felt for his pulse. It was weak, but there. In front Hassan and As'ad were crumpled on top of each other, both having been flung against the windshield with considerable force. Hassan was moaning which meant he was alive, but As'ad was silent, his head bloody.

Mark unfastened his seat belt and crawled out of the car. He could hear shouting, the sound of men jumping from the helicopter and running towards the wrecked car. *Shit...who are they?* The answer came with a sickening churning in his stomach as he looked up and saw Malouf and Fiqar standing on the edge of the gully staring down at him, triumphant smirks on their swarthy faces.

"So, Doctor Hamilton…" Malouf could barely keep the satisfaction out of his voice. "Your little escape plan has come to an unfortunate end. Are the others dead?"

"No, but they're badly hurt and need immediate medical attention," Mark shouted at them.

"A pity they will not receive it." Malouf gestured impatiently. "Come up here, Doctor…*now*."

Mark didn't move. "You can't just leave them here to die. These are Prince Rashid's attendants. He'll be —"

"They are traitors," Malouf snapped. "The prince will not want to see them again."

"Nevertheless, I'm not leaving them here without calling for help. There must be a hospital nearby."

Malouf made a gesture and two men jumped down into the gully, each one grabbing Mark by the arms and hustling him up the slope.

"Dammit, Malouf," he seethed, "you can't just leave them there. They'll die without medical attention —" He broke off at the sound of a loud engine of some kind approaching fast. Startled, the men surrounding Mark looked in that direction, but there were no headlights visible. *What the hell…?* He gasped as a black Hummer suddenly barrelled into view headed straight at them.

"Shoot!" Malouf screamed and Mark's captors released his arms as they trained their guns on the Hummer.

Jack, it must be Jack! Mark exulted, then punched the nearest man's arm just as he fired. Fiqar shrieked and fell to the ground writhing, his legs shredded by the bullets from the man's gun. Cursing, Malouf grabbed at Mark but missed as he danced out of reach.

"Jack!" he yelled, running towards the Hummer he could only hope like hell was being driven by the man he'd wished for. Bullets whizzed and whined past his ears as the Hummer came to a screeching stop.

"Get in!" Jack had the passenger door already open and Mark dived inside. Jack threw the vehicle into reverse, backing up into the darkness at high speed.

"Jack…" Mark stared at his lover in awe. "I can't believe you could do this again. How did you know where I was?"

"I have ways," Jack replied tersely. "Keep your head down 'til I get this fucker turned around. They're not going to let us get away without a fight."

"Jack…" Mark slid down in his seat and buckled up. "The guys who helped me escape, they're back there, badly hurt. We need to get them some help."

"Are you nuts?" Jack's eyes widened as he stared at Mark. "Those wankers nearly had you killed." He snorted. "Escape? That was the worst escape plan I've ever seen."

"But they need help, Jack. I can't just abandon them."

"Jesus…" Yanking hard on the steering wheel, Jack brought the Hummer around, sand and loose stones swirling into the air under the tires. He handed Mark his cell phone. "Here…call the operator and get connected to the local hospital. Tell them they need to send an ambulance to Rashid's estate. Warn them there are armed men there, and they need to alert the police. That's the best we can do for right now."

Mark nodded and punched in the number for the operator. As they bumped and rolled over the rutted road he explained to an attendant at the hospital what was needed and that they'd better inform the police of the situation. The roar of rotors overhead signalled they were being pursued by Malouf and his gang. A burst of gunfire kicked up the sand all around the Hummer. Jack stomped on the brake, bringing the Hummer to an abrupt halt, and the chopper shot past them.

"Take the steering wheel," Jack shouted. Opening his door, he jumped out and ran in front of the Hummer. Mark slid into the driver's seat and gunned the engine. Jack grabbed one of the AK47's he'd taken from Malouf's men back in Khartoum, firing at the chopper as it turned and headed back their way.

"You hit it!" Mark yelled, seeing the helicopter dip then veer off to the side.

Jack jumped in alongside him. "*Go*," he yelled. "There's a trail up the side of the cliff about a mile ahead. Take that." He stuck his head out the window. "They're coming back—slow down when I give you the word."

"Right." Mark peered ahead, looking for the trail Jack had indicated, his knuckles white as he gripped the steering wheel hard.

"Here they come…" Jack was hanging out the window, gun trained on the chopper as it gained on them. "Right, slow down, Doc…let 'em get ahead of us."

Mark applied pressure on the brake, almost ducking when the chopper roared over them. He heard the rapid burst from Jack's gun, then Jack yelling, "Gotcha, ya bastard!" Mark stared into the rear view mirror and yelped happily as he saw smoke pour from underneath the chopper. There was no explosion, but the chopper fell behind, obviously losing power.

"Okay, full speed ahead," Jack yelled, "and watch for that turn."

"Got it," Mark said, grinning. "You're the man, Jack." He turned the Hummer onto the trail and hit the gas pedal hard. When they reached the top of the cliff, Jack told him to slow, then stop.

"Let's see what's happenin' down there." He jumped out and peered through his binoculars at Rashid's estate far below. The sun was coming up, casting enough light for him to see Malouf's helicopter had managed a forced landing near Rashid's home.

"Looks like they got an ambulance there to take care of your buddies," he told Mark. "Wait..." He could also see some vehicles that looked familiar, and at the coastline a transport carrier. "Well, I'll be damned..."

"What is it?" Mark asked.

"Looks like old Rashid's family sent him a calling card."

"What?"

"Those are Saudi security guards taking Malouf and his gang into custody. But how'd they manage to get in on this?"

"Hassan said something about having things taken care of," Mark told him. "He also said he and his brother, Omar, were supposed to be returned to their family after a year serving Rashid. It didn't happen, so maybe he told his folks to get in touch with the authorities?"

"Could be..."

"Let's go back down there, Jack. I want to make sure the boys are all right."

Jack groaned. "I could've bet ten quid you were going to say that."

"Please, Jack..."

Sighing, Jack pulled Mark into his arms. "All right, Doc...but if it looks dicey, we're not staying. Got that?"

"Got it..." Mark grinned up at the handsome sergeant and pressed their groins together. "Mmm...going to get this too, later."

"If you're a good boy," Jack teased, taking Mark's bottom lip between his. Mark opened to him, and the kiss they shared had a hint of desperation. "Want you," Jack breathed into Mark's mouth. "Want you so damned bad."

"Me too," Mark mumbled. "And you'll get me—after we check out the situation down there."

Three armed guards gave them the signal to stop as they approached the scene of the accident, then gestured with their guns that they should get out of the Hummer. A tall, slim and handsome man in fatigues walked over, scowling at them.

"You have business here?" he asked sharply.

"You could say that," Jack drawled. "I'm Sergeant Major Jack Caruthers, UN Peacekeeping Task Force, and this is Doctor Mark Hamilton. He was being held hostage in Prince Rashid's fortress there. The three lads being put in that ambulance were helping him escape when Malouf's gang of cutthroats got in the way. And you are...?"

The man raised an eyebrow. "I am Prince Najid, commander of this security task force." He looked Mark up and down with an appraising eye. "So, you are the hostage I was ordered to find and send to the American Embassy in Khartoum."

"If you say so." Mark looked over at the ambulance. "How are Omar and Hassan—the boys in the car?"

Najid's eyes narrowed as if he expected a different reaction from the man he had been sent to rescue. "They will be all right. The driver was not so lucky. He's in critical condition—a broken neck, I believe."

"So, how did you happen to arrive at the scene?" Jack asked.

"Omar has been in touch with his family for some time asking that they acquire their release from Prince Rashid's service," Najid explained. "My great-uncle is a very foolish old man and would not listen to reason, so my family decided to take matters into their own hands. The boys were impatient and should have waited for our arrival instead of trying to engineer their own escape…"

"Maybe if you'd let them know you were on your way, they'd have waited." Mark couldn't disguise his anger. "How were they expected to know when you'd eventually show up?"

Before Prince Najid could give any answer, Mark brushed by him. "I just want to make sure they're okay," he muttered, hurrying over to the ambulance. Hassan, on his back on a gurney, stared at him through stricken eyes. His face was badly cut and bruised. Omar, who had suffered only from being badly shaken, stood by him, holding his hand.

"As'ad…" Hassan gazed at Mark and asked weakly. "Will he be all right, Doctor?"

"I don't know." Mark looked over to where the young security guard was being carefully loaded into the ambulance, his head in restraints. "Prince Najid said his neck is broken. I'll check with the paramedics…"

But the medics weren't in any mood to give out information even after Mark had told them he was a doctor. They waved Mark away, hustled the brothers into the ambulance and drove off. Shaking his head, Mark watched it leave then returned to where Jack stood talking to Najid.

Out of Najid's sightline, Jack did a quick eye roll at Mark. "His Highness here tells me they're taking Prince Rashid back home where he'll be cared for properly."

"He shouldn't be moved for another couple of days," Mark cautioned.

Najid raised an aristocratic eyebrow. "You still care for his health, Doctor, after what he tried to do to you?"

"He's an old man." Mark shrugged. "Kinda sad, really."

Najid snorted. "He is a despicable old man who has wasted his life in degeneracy. My family should have put a stop to this years ago."

"What will happen to him?"

"As you said, Doctor, he is an old man. He will live out the rest of his life under watchful eyes."

"What about Malouf, and that asshole Fiqar?"

"Under arrest. Fiqar will need medical treatment..." Najid's eyes grew cold. "But that can wait—"

The sounds of angry voices caught their attention. Malouf and his gang were not going quietly. Malouf glared over at Jack and Mark. "You think you have beaten me," he yelled at them as Najid's men struggled to control him, "but it's not over between us. I will hunt you down—both of you. You cannot hide from me!"

"Ah, belt up, Malouf," Jack growled. "You'll be an old man by the time they let you out of the bloody jail, if ever."

Mark shuddered as he watched the big Turk being forced into one of the security vehicles. Malouf gave them one last sinister look before he disappeared from their sight. "Let's go, Jack," Mark said grimly. "I have a sudden need to get as far away as we possibly can from all this."

* * * *

They found a resort town on the coast and checked in to a hotel on the beach. Mark couldn't help being amazed that the small country of Eritrea, surrounded on all sides by countries engaged in civil strife and rebellion, enjoyed a brisk tourist trade and strong economy. If the hotel receptionist who registered them was surprised by Mark and Jack's ragged and road stained appearances, he said nothing, but took his time to carefully double-check the credit card Jack handed over for the night's stay. He'd called Major Holbrook at the base earlier to tell him Doctor Hamilton was safe and sound, and would he kindly inform all interested parties of the fact—especially Ghali?

"That kid will be doin' jumpin' jacks when he hears you're all right," Jack had said after finishing his conversation with the Major.

"Yeah... God, Jack, how many ways can I thank you for coming after me, *again*. You really are my knight in shining armour—well, slightly dusty armour right now."

They had laughed together and Mark had snuggled against Jack's side as they'd sped up the coast, away from corrupt princes and bad guy slavers, hopefully never to run into the likes of them again.

* * * *

"Wow, Jack, this is great." Mark looked around the spacious room decorated in shades of blue and white. "Look at that bed, will ya?" He grinned at Jack. "King size, yippee. At last!"

Jack chuckled and pulled him into his arms. He nuzzled Mark's neck, then caught his lips in a blistering kiss. His hands roamed over Mark's body as he began peeling off his clothes.

"Shower," Mark gasped, his blood instantly on fire from Jack's touch. "If I have ever needed a shower more than now, I can't remember the occasion."

"Too right..." Jack shucked off his fatigues and marched Mark into the bathroom. "Shower, then lots of grub. I'm famished." He turned on the hot spray.

"But what comes in between?" Mark teased.

"What d'you think?" Jack growled, shoving Mark ahead of him into the shower stall.

"Oh boy, feels so good." Mark raised his face to the hot water then grabbed the shampoo and slapped a liberal amount on his hair. Jack stood behind him, massaging Mark's scalp, working up a lather, hands moving down to gently knead his neck and shoulders. Mark's head fell back as he gave himself up to Jack's ministrations. He pushed his rump into the heat and hardness of Jack's groin, revelling in the feel of the thick cock wedged between his butt cheeks. His hands slid round to cup Jack's firm ass, pulling him in even closer, wriggling his own ass over the hard pulsing flesh.

"God, Jack, I have missed you like I've never missed anyone before in my life." He hesitated, then said quietly, "A shower stall may be a strange place to say this for the first time, but—I love you."

Jack wrapped his arms tightly round Mark's lithe body and nuzzled his neck. "Love you too," he murmured. "Have since our first time together."

Mark turned in Jack's embrace and placed his lips on Jack's. "Why didn't you say it?"

"Wanted to hear you say it first." Jack's piercing blue gaze fixed on Mark. "I didn't want you to think I was rushing you." His voice was husky with emotion."You know, making a claim I had no right to."

"You've every right to. More than anyone in the world, you have that right. I love you, Jack. I always will."

Their kiss was one of sweet commitment laced with a hungry desire that brought a growl from deep in Jack's throat and a whimper of need from Mark. Untangling himself from Jack's arms he fell to his knees and took the mass of Jack's throbbing cock between his lips, letting the pre cum pool on his tongue. He teased the sensitive underside of Jack's cock head with the tip of his tongue before taking as much of the thick shaft as he could into his mouth. Jack groaned, his hands smoothing Mark's wet hair off his face, caressing his neck and shoulders. Mark gripped Jack's cock at the base and pumped it in and out of his mouth, slowly at first, his tongue swirling up and down the length of the hot rigid flesh, then with an urgency that had Jack moaning out loud. Mark's free hand slid between Jack's muscular thighs, caressing his balls, feeling them pull up tight as the big man shuddered, and with a strangled groan, released a torrent of cum into Mark's eager mouth.

Mark gulped at the warm, salty cream, swallowing it down, relishing the tangy taste, holding Jack's pulsing cock until every drop was wrung from him.

Jack lifted Mark to his feet and held him in a bone popping embrace. Their lips met in another long, searing kiss, tongues seeking every corner of each other's mouths, the slick flesh tussling and meshing inside their moist heat. Gasping they pulled apart, gleaming eyes on one another, reflecting the need building within them.

"Let's get outta here," Jack muttered. Quickly they rinsed each other off then cut the shower spray. Jack grabbed a towel from the rack and wrapped it around Mark, gently rubbing it over his skin. Only partly dry, they backed one another up into the bedroom and fell on the bed. Jack covered Mark's body with his own, scouring Mark's smooth, damp skin with hot, hungry kisses that had Mark writhing in ecstasy under him. He attacked Mark's nipples, one by one, teasing them with his lips and teeth while his hands roamed over Mark's body, stroking and caressing the firm, lightly muscled flesh, bringing small gasps and moans of pleasure from Mark's parted lips.

Jack's kisses travelled south until the head of Mark's erection nudged his cheek. His lips encircled the glistening head, his tongue flicking over the velvety flesh, scooping up the copious pre cum oozing from the slit.

"Yeah…" His sigh of appreciation was followed by him making a long, slow glide down the length of Mark's cock, all the way to the thatch of blond hair, where he buried his nose to inhale Mark's scent, a clean, musky fragrance that drove him slightly mad with lust. His fingers stroked Mark's balls then strayed over his perineum, circling Mark's tight opening, one finger pushing gently until the resisting muscle yielded, and his finger slipped inside Mark's silken heat. He was rewarded by Mark's pleasured cry and the arching of his young, supple body against Jack's own hard torso. Jack's lips tightened their pressure on Mark's cock, relentlessly sliding up and down the rock hard flesh that pulsed and throbbed in his mouth.

Mark's moans and the quickening of his breath told Jack he was close to coming, and as much as he wanted to fuck Mark, his desire to feel the rush and taste of Mark's cum in his mouth won out. There would be time... He increased the power of his sucking, his tongue swirling all around Mark's cock. His lover's body writhed and bucked under him, his hands clutched at Jack's head, his fingers skimming over the close cropped hair. Then shouting Jack's name he came, the taste and scent of his cum filling Jack's mouth, searing his senses with an overload of sensation so intense, it momentarily dizzied him. He held Mark gently until the spasms eased and his breathing calmed, then he released his cock with a final lick over the head, and stretched out over Mark's welcoming body, finding his lips eagerly waiting to be kissed.

"Love you, Jack..."

"Love you too, Doc...Mark," he corrected himself with a grin.

Mark kissed the tip of Jack's nose. "You can call me anything you like, as long as you love me."

"No fear of that ending any time soon," Jack murmured. "'Fraid you're stuck with me, like it or not."

"I like it." He ground his crotch against Jack's and gave him a lascivious smile. "You gonna fuck me now, or did I wear you out already?"

"Saucy little devil, aren't you?"

"Insatiable little devil, actually, when it comes to you." He grinned and reached under the pillow, producing a small bottle of bath oil. "I found this in the bathroom, and thought it might save my poor ass next time you felt like fucking the daylights out of me."

They chuckled together, then Jack took the oil and smeared it on his fingertips. Mark lifted his butt, giving Jack access, and sighed with satisfaction when Jack inserted one then two fingers deep inside him.

"Oh yeah, Jack…" He squirmed over the thrilling invasion, pulling Jack down for a long, passionate kiss. Using his knees Jack opened Mark's legs wide, then lifted them around his waist. He pushed forward, the head of his cock penetrating beyond the ring of muscle that briefly resisted his invasion. A gasp of pleasured pain escaped from Mark's lips, his breath filling Jack's mouth.

Jack slid into Mark's heat, pulled back then plunged back in, deeper this time, starting a rocking rhythm that had Mark moaning out loud, and clinging to Jack's hard body as though he would never let him go. Each thrust from Jack's powerful pelvis, each pass of his rock hard cock over Mark's prostrate brought Mark such exquisite pleasure, it bordered on the unbearable. Mark's eyes were scrunched tight, his hands slid up and down over Jack's sweat slicked torso, his hips arched upward, moving to match his lover's deliciously slow but forceful thrusts.

"Jack, oh yes, Jack…"

Mark's moans quickened Jack's pace. Groaning from deep inside his chest, he rammed into Mark, harder, faster. His body stiffened over Mark's, his tongue spearing Mark's mouth as passion overwhelmed him and the onrush of his orgasm set his blood on fire. He reached for Mark's throbbing erection, pumping it quickly, roughly, bringing him to a gasping climax. As Mark's hot seed spilled over his hand, Jack came in long body-racking spasms that left him spent and breathless, his chest heaving as if he'd run a twenty-mile marathon.

"Holy shit, Doc..." Jack sat back on his heels, pulling Mark up onto his lap to keep them joined as one. Mark wrapped his arms around Jack's neck, pressing their sweat-soaked bodies together. His lips scoured Jack's mouth while he moved his hips sensuously over Jack's still hard cock.

"Love you, Jack," he whispered against his lover's lips. "Love you with everything I've got to give."

Jack's rasping sigh and the tightening of his arms around Mark's body was all the assurance Mark needed.

* * * *

Later, they showered again, then ordered room service. They shared a celebratory bottle of wine, clinking their glasses together and wishing Malouf and his cutthroats a long prison sentence.

"Jack..." Mark looked thoughtful after he'd sipped his wine. "What about Ghali?"

"Yeah, little tyke needs a home."

"Exactly what I was thinking. Maybe we should look into ways we could take him with us."

There was a pregnant pause, then Jack said quietly, "And where exactly are 'us' going?"

"Well, Australia, of course." Mark raised a blond eyebrow. "You're not reneging on your offer are you?"

Jack's face was split by the biggest smile Mark had ever seen on him. "I should bloody well think not!" He jumped to his feet, almost knocking over the table they were sitting at. "Bloody hell...!" He swept Mark into his arms and gave him a resounding kiss. "That's the best bit of news I've ever had."

"Well, honestly, Jack," Mark said with a laugh, "isn't it a bit ridiculous to think you and I could live on opposite sides of the world after all we've been through together?"

"No, we couldn't—and we won't." He kissed Mark again. "So all we have to do is get a visa for the kid — that is, of course, if the little fella wants to come with us."

Mark slipped his hands inside Jack's robe and caressed the warm, smooth skin of his torso, relishing the feel of muscle rippling under his touch. "Yeah, the decision has to be his," he said, trying not to let the sensuous feel of Jack's smooth skin under his fingers distract him. "But honestly, d'you think he'll say no?"

Jack nuzzled Mark's neck with his lips. "Don't think so..." He groaned softly. "You're gettin' me all fired up again."

"Then we better talk about this tomorrow." Mark's hands glided down Jack's spine to cup the twin globes of his butt.

"You're just full of bright ideas today, aren't you?"

* * * *

Despite the blissful feelings of contentment that suffused Mark's mind now that he and Jack were reunited, and it looked as though the danger Malouf represented was safely in the past, Mark couldn't help but wonder sadly of Omar and Hassan's fate. Although the boys were not entirely blameless during his captivity, they had alerted Rashid's family of his abduction, and included him in their attempt to escape. They could, after all, have simply left him behind...

"You're fretting over something." Jack's gruff voice interrupted Mark's thoughts.

"You're beginning to know me too well." Mark smiled and covered Jack's hand with his own. They were in the borrowed Hummer on their way back to the UN base. "I was just wondering about Omar and Hassan. What d'you suppose will happen to them now?"

"They'll go home, I should think."

"Hassan's in love with As'ad, the security guard who was badly injured. I wonder what will happen there..."

Jack grimaced. "Their family's not going to encourage that, I'm afraid. I'd be surprised if they ever saw one another again. You saw how that Najid geezer reacted to his uncle's escapades."

"That's different, Jack. Rashid's a dirty old man. The boys are in love..."

Jack squeezed Mark's hand gently. "Not every love story has a happy ending you know."

"I know," Mark said with a long sigh. "It doesn't make me feel any better about the situation, though. I wish I could contact their family and tell them As'ad was trying to help their sons."

"Good luck with that. Believe me, they won't want to hear from you or anyone else on the matter. Omar and Hassan will be married to suitable young ladies before they know what's happening. That's the Saudi way."

"And As'ad?"

Jack shrugged. "We don't know his background of course, but I'd say if he recovers, the same story goes for him — wife and kids."

"And assignations in the dark," Mark muttered, depressing himself at the thought of a life repressing one's true feelings for the sake of a narrow-minded society.

"Hey, it's not just here, y'know. Loads of men and women all over the world have to hide their true identities. We're just lucky, is all."

"Right, lucky." He leaned over to kiss Jack's cheek. "Very lucky…"

* * * *

Their first stop on their way back to the base was in Khartoum to return Eirik's Hummer. The young Norwegian looked surprised but grateful at having his vehicle returned, and in not too bad condition.

"I took your Jeep in for a service," he told Jack, digging out the keys from his pants' pocket as they walked out to the parking lot in back of the UN building. "It should get you wherever you're going from here." He gave Mark a careful appraising look after they'd been introduced. "You're a lucky man,

Doctor Hamilton. I don't know many men who would have gone to such extremes to rescue a friend."

Jack blushed and shuffled his feet uncomfortably under Eirik and Mark's admiring stares. "You're right, Eirik," Mark said. "I'm very lucky to have Jack in my life."

Eirik gave them both a short but almost formal bow. "Well, I wish you a good life together, whatever you do after this."

"Going to Australia," Jack told him firmly, with obvious pride. "Raise horses…"

"Sounds wonderful. I might visit you there one day."

They said their goodbyes and Mark chuckled as he watched the slim Norwegian walk away, his back ramrod straight. He pinched Jack's arm. "He has the hots for you, not that I blame him, of course."

"Naw…" Jack shook his head. "He just wanted to help me out."

"That's what I meant."

Jack swatted Mark's butt. "Get in the Jeep," he growled.

"It's okay…" Mark laughed as he climbed inside the Jeep. "I get to help you out instead."

Chapter Fourteen

Hannad Malouf stared about him through hostile, narrowed eyes. He took in the high walls of the compound he'd spent the last month in, at the barbed wire atop the walls, at the security guards who patrolled the compound day and night—and Malouf grinned, a mirthless, malicious baring of his teeth. He had just been informed he was to be released into the custody of Turkish authorities, that he and what remained of his followers were to be transported to a prison just outside Istanbul where they would await sentencing by a Turkish court.

Malouf had no intention of going to any prison, Turkish or otherwise. En route to his homeland he would escape, with or without his men. It was necessary. He would not rest until the men responsible for his present situation had paid the price for humiliating him in such a manner. The young doctor he would debase in all kinds of insidious ways. The arrogant Australian sergeant he would kill, slowly. Then he would recapture the boy, Ghali, and sell him to the highest bidder. Whatever plans they had formed for their future, he would crush and destroy...

A group of guards approached, rounding up Malouf's men, signalling that he should join them as their hands were tied and they were forced aboard a transport truck parked nearby. Malouf noticed with satisfaction that the preparations were sloppy; there were no cuffs on his wrists, only cord to bind them. Only one armed guard climbed in the back of the truck with them, while another sat up front with the driver. The Turk shook his head, and a sly smile parted his lips. This would be even easier than he thought. He grinned at the guard sitting across from him, almost sniggering at the young man's obvious nervousness. Sweat coated the man's brow, and his eyes were everywhere but on Malouf and his men.

Dhul Fiqar was not going with them. He was still somewhere in some hospital Malouf neither knew of, nor cared about. The man had proved himself less than useful, and his absence worried Malouf not at all. *Probably for the best,* he mused. Fiqar's obsession with the American doctor's beauty was a nuisance Malouf could well do without now.

His grin widened as he envisioned torturing the Australian while the young doctor watched and screamed for mercy for his lover. The young guard was openly gaping at him, and that amused Malouf even more. *The poor fool is wondering why I'm so happy going to jail. He'll soon find out...* Malouf's eyes swept over his men. There were three of them left—only three. More reasons for him to kill the Australian. But they were enough to overpower the driver and the two guards.

He waited until the compound could no longer be seen across the flat terrain, then with a speed and agility that belied his bulk, he threw his bound hands over the guard's head and pulled the surprised man into a back-breaking embrace. The guard, who had dropped his gun when Malouf attacked him, screamed for help as he struggled to free himself from Malouf's grip, but he was no match for the big Turk's size and strength.

"Get his knife," Malouf rasped and one of his men sprang to his feet, fumbling for the knife hanging from the guard's belt. Despite his bonds he managed to drag it from its sheath, then slit the cords round Malouf's wrists. "Free the others, then knock on the driver's window, and tell him to stop or I will snap this puny one in two."

The truck came to a screeching halt when the driver saw his fellow guard a captive in Malouf's arms. He and the third guard leapt from the cab and ran round to the back of the truck, guns at the ready. Malouf swung the trapped guard in front of him, then launched the terrified man and himself on top of the gunmen. The driver screamed and fired, killing Malouf's human shield instantly, but was then slammed into the ground under the weight of two bodies. Malouf's men spilled from the truck, overpowering the other guard who seemed stunned by the turn of events. He was quickly disarmed and forced to his knees.

Malouf heaved himself to his feet with a satisfied grunt. "Shoot them," he muttered, "and dispose of the bodies. We are going to Khartoum."

* * * *

Mark swore softly to himself as he heard Jack arguing with the immigration authorities at the Australian Embassy. He'd had this same conversation several times already, but officialdom refused to budge on this issue — Ghali's father could not be found to give his permission for his son to leave the country. No matter that the man had sold his son into slavery, he was still the boy's legal guardian, and until he signed a release form, Ghali could not leave with Mark and Jack.

This stalemate was delaying their departure, and although Major Holbrook had agreed to accept Jack's resignation and arrange his honourable discharge, he had allowed Jack to stay on at the base, and had allocated quarters for Mark and Ghali. This couldn't go on indefinitely, however, and each day that extended the delay only added to their frustration. At least one thing had gone right since they'd returned from Eritrea — Mark's replacement had shown up at the refugee clinic, and even if parting with Asima and the other staff had been bittersweet, Mark was filled with anticipation at starting a new life, in a new country, with Jack.

His attention was diverted from listening to Jack's telephone argument by Ghali who rushed into the room, his eyes wide with excitement, and not a little fear.

"Doctor Mark, Doctor Mark," he cried, tugging on Mark's arm. "Bad men are attacking the base — !" As if to emphasise his warning a loud explosion erupted nearby and the ground shook under their feet.

"What the—?" Jack flung the phone down and ran to the door. "Fuckin' rebels," he yelled over his shoulder at Mark after scanning the airspace immediately over the base. "Who'd have thought they'd have the balls to—" Another explosion rocked the building, and bits of ceiling tile showered down on Mark and Ghali. "Let's go!" Jack hefted Ghali into his arms then grabbed Mark, hustling him outside. Two heavily armed AH-64 Apache helicopters were circling the base, each sending down a barrage of deadly fire from their nose mounted auto-cannons. The well-drilled Aussie soldiers were quick to recover from this surprise attack, countering the rebel fire with a disciplined machine gun strike, spewing out a lethal hail of bullets that had one chopper veering off sharply, smoke pouring from its belly.

"Sarge—over here!" Paddy signalled frantically from behind an armoured Jeep that served as shelter for him and three fellow soldiers.

"Take the kid," Jack ground out, pulling his Beretta M9 from its holster. "I'll cover you." Mark didn't pause to argue. He didn't want to leave Jack's side, but Ghali's safety came first at that moment. Hoisting the little guy over his shoulder, he made a mad dash for the protection of the Jeep's steel-plated sides. All around him was the deafening boom and pop of artillery, the shouts of men giving orders, and the thud of mortar fire.

"Bastards are in the perimeter," someone yelled and Mark could see a dozen or so rebels racing across the training ground in front of the barracks, firing what looked like M14s as they ran. He saw two Australian soldiers go down, then more rebels appeared and in a flash the situation changed to one of hand-to-hand combat in which Mark found himself defending himself and Ghali against desperate odds. He grabbed a fallen soldier's pistol and stopped a rebel in his tracks as he came hurtling towards them, screaming at the top of his voice. Ghali pressed himself against Mark's chest and Mark swore he could feel the terrified child's heart pounding in unison with his own.

"Good shot!" he heard Paddy yell, but then the young private disappeared behind a human wall as the rebels surrounded them, shooting indiscriminately. Holding Ghali in his arms, Mark rolled under the Jeep, desperately trying to locate Jack among the melee of fighting men, and at the same time avoid the grasping hands of the rebels as they reached under the Jeep, grabbing at him and Ghali.

"*No*," he screamed as Ghali was torn from his grasp. The boy's terrified wail resounded in Mark's ears. "No, you bastards!" Mark rolled out from under the Jeep and launched himself at the man who held the struggling Ghali in an iron grip. Ghali kicked madly at the man's shins who didn't see Mark until he was on him. Using the butt of the pistol he'd found, Mark battered the man's turbaned head, cursing him with filthy words he'd never used in his life before.

Strong hands grabbed at his shoulders and he was pulled off the unconscious rebel. Still swearing, he swung a punch at his new assailant, only to have his fist caught in a large hand, effectively blocking the blow aimed at the man's chin.

"Doc, whoa! It's me, Jack—blimey, you're a right ball of fire and no mistake. Remind me never to get on your bad side!"

Mark practically collapsed against Jack's chest. "Oh, thank god, Jack...did we win?"

"Buggers have gone, but the base is compromised. I'd love to know how they found us here."

Mark picked Ghali up, hugging him tight. "You're a brave little guy," he told him. "Did you see how he was laying into that rebel, Jack?"

Jack grinned, and ruffled Ghali's curly hair. "Just as good as you laying into him, I'd say. Fella never had a chance with you two."

Paddy and Harry came running over. "They've caught a couple of the bastards," Harry said, panting. "We might be able to find out from them how they knew about the base."

"And there's this one here." Jack dug the toe of his boot into the fallen rebel's ribs. "Wait a mo'..." He leaned over the groaning man for a closer look. "Doesn't this one look familiar?" he asked Mark.

Mark took a closer look. "Shit...it's one of Malouf's men. How in hell did he get all the way out here?"

At the mention of Malouf's name Ghali's eyes widened, and his little body stiffened in Mark's arms. "Bad men come for me..."

"No, Ghali," Mark said firmly. "They're not getting anywhere near you again. I promise."

Jack hauled the dazed man to his feet. "*Ayna Malouf?*" he snarled, his face inches from the slaver's. "Where is he?"

"He must've escaped from the Saudi security," Mark muttered when the man refused to answer. "But why would he be in league with the rebels?"

"To get his hands on—" Jack stopped himself from saying the obvious and scaring Ghali unnecessarily, but Mark's heart sank at the thought that Malouf knew where he and Ghali were, and could get this close to recapturing them.

"Jack, we have to get Ghali away from here, *now*."

Jack nodded. "I'll go talk to the Major."

* * * *

Despite the heavy fire inflicted on the base, casualties were surprisingly light. Only one army fatality, and five injured. A couple of rebel bodies were found among the bushes on the base's perimeter, the wounded apparently having escaped. The three captives were questioned but were not talking, so far. The biggest problem was now security had been breached and their position known, the UN would order them to relocate—not something that could be done overnight. All Jack and Mark could see from this latest setback were more delays in getting Ghali out of the country, and harm's way—more essential now than ever with Malouf back in the picture.

"The Major's up to his eyeballs right now with more problems than us," Jack said after his meeting with Holbrook. He watched as Mark attended to one of the wounded soldiers at the base clinic. Mark had volunteered his services to help out the medical staff after the attack. "However… and we're really going to have to buy him a pint or three when this is all over…he's going to give the three of us passage to Al Fashir on the first chopper convoy out of here."

"Fantastic." Mark finished bandaging the soldier's sutured bicep, then asked, "When's that happening?"

"Oh-seven-hundred tomorrow. I reckon we can get to Cairo from there without a problem. I'll tackle the Australian Embassy there, and I'm thinking maybe you should talk to somebody at the American Embassy. If we can just maybe get the okay to take him overseas for a holiday, we could work on extending his stay — get ourselves a lawyer..."

"My brother's a lawyer in Queensland." The soldier Mark had been attending to sat up and grinned at them. "Thanks, Doc, by the way... Yeah, he'd be glad to help once you get the kid there."

"It's getting him there that's the problem." It seemed everyone on the base knew of Ghali's plight, and that realisation suddenly gave Mark a shiver of discomfort.

"What?" Jack asked.

Mark smiled at the soldier and patted his shoulder. "Thanks for the offer — and your arm will be fine in a couple of days." He steered Jack towards the clinic exit. "How would Malouf know that Ghali was here?" he asked quietly. "Or me, for that matter? For all he knew, I might have gone back to the refugee clinic. Somebody must be feeding him information — somebody on the base."

Jack frowned and shook his head. "Not one of our lads, but we do have some locals working here, helping load transports, engine maintenance, that kind of thing."

"And Malouf's got the kind of money that could get him information."

"So if someone is in his pay, he'll know where we're off to tomorrow. But why the hell is he going to all this trouble to get at you and Ghali? He's got to know if he's caught again it's a life sentence. I mean..." Jack lowered his voice, "You're a cracker, Doc, but it's not like he's tried to get in your pants, has he? If it's the money, there's loads of other likely candidates out there..."

"Revenge," Mark said. "He's pissed we managed to get away, twice, and we're the reason he got arrested. A man like Malouf doesn't forgive and forget. He wants to get a hold of Ghali to teach us a lesson, and if he gets to me again, he'd probably get a kick out of selling me to some dung farmer or something, just to see me squirm."

"Over my fucking dead body," Jack growled.

"And don't think that's not part of his plan." Mark took Jack's arm and led him outside. "We need to get out of here without anyone knowing where we're going."

"You mean hijack a chopper?" Even Jack's eyes widened at the thought.

"Not necessarily a helicopter—a Jeep maybe. We'll leave it someplace it can be picked up later."

"You're serious."

"Well, who can we trust here?"

"Just about any of the lads, the Major, Paddy, Harry…"

"Okay, I guess I'm being paranoid, but us leaving on convoy will be like taking out a page in the 'let's tell Malouf where we're going gazette'."

"Right…" Jack was silent for a moment. "Okay," he said finally, "I'll fill the Major in, see what he suggests. Much as I love you Doc, stealing Australian Army vehicles is not on the list of things I swore I'd do for you."

* * * *

Malouf stared about him in disgust. He'd lost yet another man, and the rebels' initial fiery resolve seemed to have been extinguished by the fierce retaliation of the Australian soldiers. The rebel leader had refused to mount another attack on the base, arguing it was too well garrisoned and defended. Even another of Malouf's offered bribes didn't impress him enough to rally his men. Malouf was enraged enough to shoot the man, but controlled himself, knowing as undisciplined as the rebels were, they probably wouldn't let Malouf gun down their leader in front of them.

What now? he wondered. His options were few. Prince Rashid was of no further use to him. Fiqar was in a prison hospital, and therefore of no use either. He had other connections in Khartoum and Istanbul, even in Cairo, but would they assist him in his plan that would now amount to nothing more that the lust for revenge in their eyes? And Malouf wanted that revenge—needed it to satisfy the dishonour he felt had been meted out to him by the Australian, and the American doctor. As for Ghali, that little wretch had caused him this problem in the first place, running away from him, finding protection among the infidels. The boy would be punished, just as the other two would be, but Ghali's punishment would last a lifetime. He would never be free again once he, Malouf, had secured him in the special place he had chosen for him.

The boy would rue the day he had turned his back on his own family, and as for the Australian sergeant and his doctor lover, there was nowhere they could hide from him.

Chapter Fifteen

Cairo, one week later

Mark gazed out through the window of the hotel suite he, Jack and Ghali had occupied since they'd arrived in the bustling city of Cairo two days earlier. Since then they'd been in constant contact with both the Australian and American embassies, and amazingly they were, at last, having some success in their bid to get Ghali an exit visa.

They had called everyone in officialdom they thought might be able to help, at the UN, the DCI, haranguing anyone who would listen, telling them of the terrible conditions Ghali would be returned to if they didn't help. Even Eirik, the UN employee who had loaned Jack his Hummer, had pitched in to help by talking to anyone he thought might have some influence. Mark had phoned his father who, after listening to his son's hair-raising story, had promised to call every Senator he knew personally.

Slowly but surely, the obstacles to Ghali finally getting that visa were falling by the wayside, one by one.

Mark stiffened as he caught sight of a familiar looking figure in the crowded street below. No, it couldn't be...not here, not after all they'd gone through to evade this man... *Malouf.* He must be mistaken, he thought. Tall, burly men wearing robes and a fez were not uncommon in Cairo, after all. *It can't have been him...*

He turned from the window as Jack and Ghali barrelled into the room, back from a bazaar where Jack had seen a carving of a water bison he was sure his father would admire.

"What's wrong?" Jack asked, seeing the uncertainty behind Mark's welcoming smile.

"Nothing..." He made a small signal indicating he didn't want to say anything in front of Ghali. "Did you find the carving?"

"Yep. Got it right here." He slid it out of its wrapping, holding it up for Mark to see.

"Beautiful... Ghali..." Mark ruffled the boy's hair affectionately. "Maybe you should take a nap before dinner?"

"Not tired," Ghali said, yawning. "Papa Jack say we can watch TV."

"Did he...?" Mark grinned at the boy. "Well, you can watch it in your room in bed." Ghali had started calling them Papa Jack and Papa Mark as it was the most natural thing in the world for him to do. Mark thought it an improvement on Sergeant Jack and Doctor Mark, and as they had talked of eventually formally adopting Ghali one day, it was good the boy already thought of them as his guardians.

Ghali threw him a stubborn look but Jack swept him up, hoisting him onto his broad shoulders, then zig-zagging his way across the room, Ghali screeching with delight.

"Great, wake him up why don't you?" Mark muttered, smiling all the same at his lover's antics. He looked out the window again, narrowing his eyes at the milling crowd in the streets, but saw no sign of the man he feared and hated. Feared because of what he might do to Ghali should he ever catch up with them, hated because of what he was, a trafficker in human souls.

"He'll be asleep shortly." Jack was behind him, arms encircling his waist, lips nuzzling his neck. "What did you see out there?"

Mark shook his head. "I don't want to be an alarmist, but I thought I saw Malouf out there in the street earlier."

"You sure?"

"No, I'm not sure. It looked like him, but so many guys down there dress alike."

"Did it look like he was casing the hotel?"

"Not really. He didn't look up here or anything."

Jack grunted and kissed Mark's neck. "That's good then, but just to make sure, I'll go walkabout…"

"No, Jack. I don't want you taking any risks right now." He turned in his lover's arms to face him. "We're so close to finally getting Ghali his visa and flying the hell out of here. Let's forget about Malouf and concentrate on making this work. I want us gone from here…"

"I know." Jack held Mark tight to his body. "I would just feel easier if I knew for sure it wasn't that arsehole you saw. We can't let our guard down."

Mark sighed and pressed his face into the warmth of Jack's neck. "This nightmare has got to end soon."

"It will, one way or the other. But I swear to you if Malouf comes anywhere near you or Ghali, it'll be all over for him. He doesn't get to threaten us anymore."

* * * *

One day later they received a call from the American Embassy. *Would they please attend a meeting with the immigration officer at ten the following day?*

"Will we ever!" Mark yelled with excitement when he'd put the phone down. He picked Ghali up and danced him around the room. "This is it, I know it is," he crowed, holding Ghali over his head, making the boy laugh with delight. "Let's celebrate tonight, Jack."

"Whoa, whoa...let's wait until we know what the verdict is," Jack cautioned. "I don't want to get our spirits up just to have them tell us no can do."

"I'm sure it's okay this time," Mark said, hugging Ghali. "They wouldn't ask us to come in, they'd just write us a letter. Wouldn't they?"

"Well, let's just wait and see. But..." Jack wrapped his arms around both of his men. "No harm in goin' out for a nosh instead of sitting in here like we've been doing for the last few days."

The three of them must present a strange sight to the average Egyptian, Mark thought as they walked through the crowded streets of Cairo. The big, dark-haired man with the piercing blue eyes, the blond American, and the small Arab boy who skipped between them holding each man by the hand. He was aware of the many stares cast their way, and he tightened his grip on Ghali's hand, alert to the fact that while they remained in this part of the world, there was always the chance Malouf, or one of his henchmen, could attempt yet another kidnapping.

Trying to push those scary thoughts from his mind, he smiled down at Ghali's upturned face and marvelled at the amazing change in the boy's personality in the past few weeks. No more the sad child he'd been when he arrived at the clinic. Now he was proving himself to be the fun loving boy he perhaps had been when his mother was still alive, before his father saw fit to sell him to Malouf. If he lived forever, Mark felt he would never understand what had possessed the man to do such a heinous thing. To sell his own child, to never see him again for the sake of a few coins, was to Mark, and he was sure to most rational people, the most callous thing a human could do to another.

As for Malouf…the trafficker of human bodies and souls, no punishment was enough for the likes of him, Mark thought. He could only hope the man he imagined he'd seen the day before was well and truly locked up, awaiting the toughest sentence a judge could hand down.

"Here we are…" Jack steered them in the direction of a street cafe. "Best koshary in all Cairo, so the bellman at the hotel told me."

"Will I like it?" Mark asked warily. He'd never heard of koshary.

"'Course you will," Jack replied confidently. "It's the Egyptian version of Italian. Pasta, really. You'll like it." He held the door open for them and Mark appreciated the coolness inside mixed with the scent of exotic spices. They were shown to a small window table and Jack ordered a beer. Mark asked for a white wine and an orange juice for Ghali. Contrary to so many Islam countries, booze was in plentiful supply in Egypt. Jack then ordered koshary for them. The waiter – who, as it turned out, was the owner – seemed delighted they were ordering the traditional Egyptian meal.

"He thought we were tourists looking for a burger, I bet," Jack remarked, his eyes scanning the street outside.

"You looking for someone?" Mark asked innocently.

"Just keeping my eyes open for any unwanted visitors. I haven't forgotten what you mentioned yesterday."

Ghali looked from Mark's concerned expression to Jack. "Bad men are here?" His light voice was querulous.

"No, they're not," Mark said quickly. "They are all locked up good and tight."

"My Uncle Hannad is very bad man. He took me from my father."

Jack and Mark exchanged looks of alarm. "Hannad..." Jack gave Ghali his full attention. "Hannad Malouf is your uncle?"

Ghali nodded, his eyes cast down as if ashamed.

"Oh, my God," Mark whispered. "Your uncle was selling you to Prince Rashid..."

"Did he take you from your father by force?" Jack asked, taking the boy's small hand in his much larger one.

Ghali shook his head. "My father owed my uncle much money. I was given in payment."

So this was the story Ghali had kept to himself all this time. Poor little bleeder, Jack thought bitterly. What kind of animals would do this to a child? To one of their own! He would love to get his hands on Malouf and wring the bastard's neck, after kicking the shit out of him.

"Scuse me a sec," he said suddenly, standing and reaching for his cell phone. "I need to make a call."

"Who to?" Mark asked.

"A man I know might be able to check up on things for us. Be right back." He left before Mark could protest, walking out onto the street, punching in a number from his directory as he went.

"Steve? It's Boomer."

"Boomer. Me old mate. How the hell are ya?"

"Good, but I need your help."

"Oh, yeah?"

"You heard of a slave trafficker named Hannad Malouf?"

"That bastard. Yeah, I've heard of him. Heard about him just the other day as a matter of fact. Escaped from armed guards on his way back to Turkey for trial. Killed them all. They haven't got him yet so far."

A cold hand gripped Jack's heart as he listened. So Mark hadn't been mistaken. He most likely had seen Malouf on the street outside the hotel. Instinctively, he reached for his hidden Beretta, secreted in his shoulder holster under the light jacket he was wearing.

He fingered the butt as he said, "I need Malouf gone for good. He's a threat to me and mine."

"Okay...give me your cell number so I can reach you."

Jack recited the number, then added, "I have an interview at the American Embassy tomorrow, but call me soon as you hear anything."

"You switching allegiances?"

"No. Bit complicated, but I'll fill you in once this is done." He hung up, remembering the last time he and Steve Colson had worked together in a covert operation during their time in Iraq. The danger they'd faced had forged a deep bond between them, and even though Steve had moved on into a branch of the Australian Intelligence Bureau dealing with anti-terrorism, they'd kept in touch over the years. Jack knew he could trust Steve, and if anyone could find out Malouf's whereabouts, it was Steve Colson.

He went back into the restaurant feeling just a little more relaxed than before. He paused to watch Mark and Ghali laughing and talking together in low voices. Surely nothing could go wrong now to ruin the happiness he'd found with Mark? He and Ghali were his family now. His to protect and make sure they got a chance at happiness together.

"Hey, you," Mark called from the table. "Why so deep in thought?"

Jack was saved from a detailed explanation by the arrival of the restaurant owner carrying large plates of the famed koshary.

"Mmm, smells good," Mark said as Jack sat down at the table. He gave him a keen look. "Everything okay?"

Jack nodded and ruffled Ghali's hair. "Just talking to an old friend. Thought he might be some help with our interview tomorrow."

"And?"

"And he'll talk to people he knows." Jack, evading the real reason for his call to Steve Colson, forced a smile to his lips. "We need all the help we can get. Now, try this koshary…"

That night, after Ghali had gone to sleep in his room, they lay in their bed wrapped in each other's arms, talking in low voices of their hopes for the future. A future that would eventually take the three of them to Australia, to a rural area where Jack's dream of raising horses could be fulfilled.

"Don't think the ankle-biter's scared of horses, do you?"

Mark chuckled. "I don't think Ghali's afraid of very much at all. I have a feeling he'll love it. Of course we'll have to find him a school."

Jack tweaked Mark's left nipple. "We do have one or two schools in Australia, y'know."

"*Jack*... I meant locally. I mean how far from a town is your land?"

"Not very far. It's been a few years since I've been there, so the town's most likely spread out a bit."

Mark kissed Jack's chest gently. "So, tomorrow's a big day for us. God, I hope they don't throw any more red tape at us, Jack. I want to get Ghali out of here as quickly as possible. I want to be able to start forgetting about that moron, Malouf, seeing him in places he shouldn't be. The fact he's Ghali's uncle just makes him more of a bastard than ever. Trying to sell his own nephew to some old pervert...it just makes me so fucking mad."

"I wasn't going to tell you this,' Jack said slowly, stroking Mark's hair, "but it's probably best you're aware of what the son of a bitch has been up to. That phone call I made today was to an old mate of mine from Iraq days. He's with Central Intelligence now, and he told me Malouf escaped from armed guards taking him to Turkey for trial."

Mark's body stiffened in Jack's arms. "Oh, Christ..."

"Yeah, only reason he's on the radar is he has connections with terrorist groups. His slave trafficking seems to be a sideline to raise money for them."

"What a bastard." Mark raised glaring eyes to Jack's. "As much as I want to get out of here and know Ghali is safe, I'd like to see that s.o.b. hung by his balls…"

"Know what you mean. If it wasn't for the fact I'd be putting you and Ghali in the line of fire, I'd go after the wanker myself."

"Don't even think about it," Mark snapped, suddenly wary. "I know you could take him, but we can't let him get in the way of us leaving Cairo. Let's make sure we have Ghali's visa, and then get the hell out of here." He laid his head back down on Jack's chest with a sigh. "Please let tomorrow be a good day."

"Amen to that," Jack murmured. He tightened his arms around Mark and kissed his forehead.

"Yeah," Mark whispered. "Love you, Jack." His hand moved over Jack's hard muscled torso until he found the part of him that pulsed and throbbed in Mark's hand. "Love *you* too…"

* * * *

Before their interview at the embassy, Mark insisted they went clothes shopping. "I don't think we'll make a good impression showing up in wife-beaters and shorts," he explained to counter the protest that immediately sprang to Jack's lips.

"You going to make me wear a *tie*?" he growled.

"No…" Mark chuckled. "Though I think you'd look pretty stunning in a suit and tie. Just a sports shirt and slacks; shirt and shorts for Ghali."

Jack breathed a sigh of relief. "Last time I was all decked out like that was for my brother Steve's wedding. I sweated like a horse through the whole affair."

"I checked with the concierge, and there's a mall about two blocks from the hotel. We've got time to get there, find what we want, have lunch, then get over to the embassy."

"Okay, *boss...*" Jack rolled his eyes at Ghali. "Guess we'll have to bite the bullet, son."

Ghali giggled and wrapped his arms around Jack's waist. Jack lifted him into his arms and bussed his cheek. "But when we're in my neck of the woods, you can run naked all over the place."

"When he's not in school," Mark amended.

Both Jack and Ghali groaned in unison.

Chapter Sixteen

The American Embassy was busy, with long lines at the security checkpoints, but once through they were led into a waiting room and told that a Miss Longridge would be with them directly.

"I hope she likes us," Mark murmured, his eyes glued to the door through which Miss Longridge would enter. "Ghali, remember to smile at her," he added. "A *big* smile."

Jack put his arm round Ghali and hugged him to his side."Ghali'll charm the knickers off her, won't you, sport?"

Mark laughed out loud. "Don't answer that, Ghali — and *you* – " He pretended to glare at Jack. "Don't say things like that in front of her. I've a feeling Miss Longridge wouldn't approve of her knickers being part of your conversation."

They were still chuckling when the aptly named Miss Longridge strode into the room. Tall and angular with her hair swept back into a tight bun on the nape of her neck, she gave them a watery smile as she took her seat behind a large formica topped desk. Mark was reminded of his history teacher in junior high, Miss Oakley, who always wore her hair in this same fashion. He found himself thinking he was very glad he'd persuaded Jack to 'dress up' just a bit. He stole a sideways glance at his lover, and found that even in this austere setting, Jack could give him the start of an erection inside his new slacks.

So..." He cleared his throat and shifted in his seat as Miss Longridge opened a file and stared at it for a moment then said, her voice crisp but not unpleasant, "Sergeant Major Jack Caruthers and *Doctor* Mark Hamilton, I understand you are applying for a visa for this young man..." She glanced at the file again. "Ghali Kaya." She smiled at Ghali, and this time her smile was a deal warmer as the boy beamed at her.

Mark could almost hear Jack's smug thought— *See, I told you he'd charm the knickers off her.*

"We have some news concerning Ghali's father," she continued. "Some rather disturbing news." She cleared her throat and fixed Ghali with a sympathetic look. "Ghali, my dear, your father is dead, I'm afraid."

Mark put a comforting arm around Ghali, even though he knew this news wasn't going to make the boy burst into tears or even look sad. He merely gazed at Miss Longridge through his dark, limpid eyes. "My uncle killed him, yes?"

"We don't know who, uh, killed him, Ghali, but he *was* murdered by person or persons unknown."

"My uncle," Ghali said quietly.

"His uncle's Hannad Malouf, a slave trader and suspected terrorist," Jack told her, his voice loaded with contempt. "A majorly bad type, and certainly no fit guardian for the boy."

"On that I concur, Sergeant Major. The CIA have made us aware of Mr. Malouf's nefarious actions, and of the many warrants for his arrest. When he is finally apprehended, he will not be in a position to be anyone's guardian."

"If Malouf is Ghali's uncle, why the different last name?" Mark asked.

Miss Longridge's smile was tight. "Malouf is an alias, one of many aliases he's apparently used over the years."

Mark remained silent, but inwardly was pleased Ghali wouldn't have to share the last name of a man he had come to detest more than anyone.

"But to get to the business on hand…" Miss Longridge tapped the file page she had opened. "We have conferred with the CIA and it's their opinion that Ghali, in order to keep him safe from Mr. Malouf, should be granted a temporary visa, and the two of you temporary guardianship of the boy."

"Temporary…what does that mean?" Jack commented sourly.

"It means the opposite of permanent, Sergeant Major," Miss Longridge said tartly. "It means you may take Ghali to the US, or to Australia if you prefer — we have discussed this with the Australian Consul, and they will honour the visa. Ghali will need a passport of course, but we can take care of that…"

"But what about the long term?" Jack pushed. "The kid needs a home, family, education, that kind of thing."

"And permanency," Mark added. "We appreciate what you've done for Ghali, Miss Longridge, but in order to give him the kind of life he deserves, we need to be able to plan ahead for him."

"I understand, Doctor Hamilton, but this is all I can do for the time being. Of course," she added with a small smile, "you will be free to apply for permanent residency on his behalf before his visa expires."

"Which we'll ruddy well do," Jack muttered.

Miss Longridge rose from her desk. "So, if you'll follow me to our legal department, we'll start the process immediately."

* * * *

Their shared mood was light as they stepped off the elevator on their floor. Jack's cell rang and he paused to check caller ID.

Steve Colson…

"Yeah, Steve?"

"Just wanted to give you a heads up, Boomer. Malouf's been seen in Cairo."

"Shit."

"Yeah, keep you guard up. You armed?"

"Yeah. Thanks for the info."

"We're sending out agents now, but be careful."

"Will do."

Mark, walking in front of Jack and unaware of the conversation, smiled as he watched Ghali skip ahead down the corridor to their hotel room. Yes, he exulted quietly, in three or four days the three of them would be winging their way to Australia. Mark felt a thrill of excitement course through him at the thought of Jack and him running a horse breeding station, while Ghali at last would have the life he deserved, far from those who would do him harm. Of course, there were still obstacles ahead of them—changing Ghali's temporary status to permanent was just one of them, but Mark was sure it could be done with the help of his family, and Jack's, and anyone else he could drag into the fray...

"Hold up, Ghali," Jack, catching up with Mark, suddenly called out.

Mark looked at him quizzically. "What's wrong?" Then he saw it. The door to their room was slightly ajar. "Ghali, no!"

Jack darted forward, trying to stop Ghali entering the room, but it was too late. The boy bounded inside and came face to face with Hannad Malouf who grabbed him by the throat and spun him around, gloating at Mark's horrified expression.

"Don't even try to reach for your gun, Sergeant Major Caruthers," Malouf hissed, holding Ghali as a shield. "One move I do not like and I will snap the little weasel's neck." He gestured at one of the two men by his side. "Hand my man your gun, carefully. No false moves or the boy dies."

"You fuckin' scumbag wanker," Jack muttered, but opened his jacket to reveal his holstered pistol. Malouf's thug grabbed it, pulled it free, then handed it to his compatriot.

"Search him for other weapons," Malouf ordered, and Jack stood visibly seething, but immobile while the man frisked him, running hands that looked like they hadn't seen soap and water in months over Jack's body.

Mark gritted his teeth, but knew that to enrage Malouf would be a mistake. Perhaps the man would be open to bargaining... "Malouf, if it's money you want, I can get if for you," he said, keeping his voice low and calm. "My father is wealthy, and—"

Malouf's laughter sent a chill down Mark's spine. "Oh, Doctor," he sneered. "There was a time when that might have appealed to me, but your fate is already sealed. You and Ghali have been sold to the highest bidder. You have no bartering powers I'm afraid. It is all arranged. As for your lover, here..." He paused to chuckle quietly... "A more uncomfortable fate awaits him." He turned his beady eyes on Jack. "Yes, Sergeant Major, I have devised an amusing death for you. Amusing for me and my men, that is. Not so good for you."

"Malouf, please..." Mark realised he wasn't above begging for their freedom and their lives. "Whatever you have sold us for, I will double, if you will just let us go—all three of us."

"No deal, Doctor Hamilton." He gestured again and the man who had taken Jack's gun now produced a length of cord and slipped behind Jack ready to tie his hands. He yanked Jack's arms behind his back then began winding the cord around Jack's wrists.

Mark wasn't quite sure when the squealing began, but his eyes widened as he saw the man who was attempting to tie Jack up suddenly double over, his face contorted with pain. Then he realised Jack had the guy by the balls and was squeezing them hard, crushing them in his big hands. The man screeched his pain, his fists hammering at Jack's back, all to no avail. Jack wasn't about to let go, but continued twisting and wrenching the thug's gonads until with a final screech, the man passed out, falling in a crumpled heap on the floor.

"Stop him, idiot," Malouf yelled at the other man who sprang forward and straight into one of Jack's rock hard fists. He went down without a sound.

"Fools," Malouf spat, drawing a knife and holding it to Ghali's throat. "You have just sentenced the boy to death."

"Wait," Mark cried. "My offer still stands. Let Ghali go and I'll get you the money. As much as you need, I promise."

"Mark," Jack growled. "Don't bargain with this piece of rubbish. He can't be trusted, you know that." He stepped towards Malouf. "Here's the deal, Malouf. You let Ghali go and I won't kill you. You do anything other than that, and I will tear you limb from limb—slowly."

"Infidels," Malouf spat at them. "Your arrogance knows no bounds. You think I will leave you with your dreams intact when you have done nothing but attempt to destroy and humiliate me?"

"Hey, we didn't ask you to try and fuck up our lives," Jack said, taking another step forward. "You're a slimy slave trader, a man who murdered his own brother in order to sell his son to a life that would have scarred him emotionally for life. You don't deserve to live, Malouf. I'd be doing the world a big favour if I did kill you. But like I said, let the boy go, and I'll not kill you—today."

The big Turk's chest heaved with long slow breaths, and for the first time he felt the tingle of real fear in his bowels. With both of his men out of action, he was at a disadvantage and he knew it. If he followed through on his threat to kill Ghali, the Sergeant Major would undoubtedly take him apart. If he gave the boy up, there was a chance he might still be killed. Those ice cold blue eyes the Australian fixed on him told Malouf just what the man was capable of.

"What about the money?" he asked finally, angry with himself that his voice sounded quite so querulous.

"No money," Jack said with a dismissive wave of his hand. "Just your life, Malouf. Take it or leave it. Give me Ghali and I will let you live."

"How do I know you speak the truth?"

"You don't, but I'd advise you to find out the easy way. Let Ghali go, now."

Malouf seethed with rage and uncertainty. They had beaten him again, or so they thought. If only he'd had more men at his disposal, these foreigners would not now be holding the ace cards. But because of them his resources had been cut off, his men killed or disabled. Once again, cold rage coursed through his blood. No, they would not win this time!

Cursing under his breath, he backed away from Jack, the cold steel of his knife pressing into Ghali's neck.

Jack advanced on him. "I'm warning you, Malouf..."

With a guttural cry, Malouf threw Ghali aside, sending the boy sprawling. Malouf blundered forward, head down, his massive frame acting almost as a battering ram, slamming into Jack's chest with tremendous force. The impetus sent Jack staggering backwards until he crashed against the hotel room wall. The whole room shook from the collision of the men's bodies. Malouf's bulk pinned Jack in place while one hand reached for Jack's throat, the other still holding his knife, poised to strike.

Mark cried out a warning, but Jack already had a grip on Malouf's wrist, using all his strength to wrest the knife from his hand. Malouf swore and screeched as the pain caused him to release the knife before his bones were snapped. It dropped to the floor, and before Mark could stop him, Ghali had rushed forward, picked it up and stabbed Malouf in the upper thigh. The Turk screamed and jumped back, almost knocking Ghali over, but Mark swept the boy into his arms out of harm's way. A thudding punch to Malouf's chin from Jack's balled-up fist had him momentarily reeling, then with another screech of rage he launched himself at Jack.

Mark was distracted by the sound of a moan from one of the men Jack had laid out earlier. The man was on his hands and knees, trying to get to his feet.

"Oh no, you don't," Mark muttered, quickly putting Ghali down and picking up a pedestal lamp from an end table. He brought it down on the thug's head with a satisfying crunch, then swung it at Malouf, catching him across the shoulder blades. Jack used Malouf's startled reaction to the blow from the lamp to his advantage, ramming his knee up into Malouf's crotch, hard. Retching, the Turk doubled over, his hands clawing at Jack's shirt but finding no purchase. Suddenly he was falling, a big foot was wedged between his own, tripping him, causing him to lose balance, to pitch uncontrollably forward. The floor rushed up to meet him, his nose hitting the hard wood with sickening force.

Before Malouf could even attempt to rise, Jack placed his foot on the man's neck, applying just enough pressure to immobilise him. Jack grabbed the cord the thugs had intended to tie his hands with. "Nice of you to supply us with this," he muttered from between clenched teeth as he bent to secure

Malouf's wrists behind his back. "Mark, find something to tie those other two with, while I call the police and tell them they can come collect these three buggers..."

Ghali ran over and kicked Malouf in the head. "That for killing my father," the boy cried, staring down at the groaning man.

"Okay, that's enough..." Mark gently pulled Ghali away from Malouf. "Help me find something to tie up these men." He couldn't blame the boy for hating Malouf. They all hated the bastard, but Ghali had seen enough violence in his short life and Mark could only wonder at the consequences of it.

Ghali nodded and followed Mark without protest, his hand curled around Mark's fingers. Using strips torn from pillowcases, Mark bound the two unconscious men while he listened with satisfaction to Jack informing the police where they could find and arrest the known terrorist and slave trafficker, Hannad Malouf. He took a deal of pleasure in watching the burly Turk unable to move from his prone position, Jack's booted foot still planted firmly on the back of Malouf's thick neck. *No more than you deserve, you son of a bitch*, he thought grimly. Maybe now the authorities would be more vigilant in making sure Malouf could not escape again.

"That's that, then." Jack closed his cell phone. "They'll be here in a few minutes, and you..." He applied a little more pressure to the back of Malouf's neck as he added, "You'll be gone for a long time, chum. Not that anyone's gonna cry over that." He grinned at Mark and Ghali as Malouf issued a stream of pain-filled muffled curses, his mouth constrained by the hard floor pressing against his lips.

* * * *

In the next few days they learned Malouf's punishment was to be even more severe than Mark had hoped for. The Saudis, furious Malouf had killed the guards taking him to stand trial in Turkey, demanded he be returned to their jurisdiction. Strangely, no one came to Malouf's aid, nor did any Turkish court deny the Saudi's demands. Jack was informed by his friend Steve Colson that the Saudi judge elected to preside over Malouf's trial had already been instructed to pass the death sentence on Malouf and his men.

"Guess we won't have to worry 'bout that wanker again," Jack remarked after receiving Steve's news.

"Much as I'm against the death penalty," Mark said, "I can't, for a moment, feel any remorse for that guy. He destroyed too many lives to expect anything less than what they're giving him."

"Right. But now we're ready for the off..." Jack smiled as Ghali ran into the room and jumped onto Mark's lap. He glanced at his watch. "Cab should be here in a few. You got everything, Ghali?"

"Yes, Papa Jack." Ghali's big eyes fixed on Jack's. "Will I really have my own horse when we get to 'stralia?"

"You bet. We'll all have our own horses, and go out exploring the Oz every day."

"When you're not in school." Mark kissed Ghali's curly hair.

Jack rolled his eyes. "Yeah, that too... Oh, almost forgot, Harry and Paddy phoned earlier. Said to tell you and the nipper 'safe trip' and all that."

"You'll miss them, won't you?"

"They'll come see us when their tour's over, I reckon."

"You're sure about all this, Jack? I mean, giving up everything you've ever known, settling down with me and Ghali on a farm..."

"A horse station," Jack corrected. "And yes, I've never been more sure of anything." He held out his arms to Ghali who jumped from Mark's lap to Jack's. "Life with the two of you looks pretty peachy to me after all we've been through. Might get a tad boring, of course. For you, I mean, after almost being a prince's love slave and all—"

"*Jack*. Close your ears, Ghali. You don't want to hear that particular story, yet."

Ghali looked from one to the other and smiled, and Mark had the uneasy feeling the boy already knew just what might have been in store for them, but for Jack's intervention. An involuntary shudder ran through his body, and he could only hope and pray Ghali's quick and bright mind had not been tainted by the events of the past few months.

Almost as though he had read Mark's mind, Jack reached for his hand and squeezed it gently. "Don't worry, Doc. Ghali's just fine, aren't you, kid?"

Ghali nodded happily then asked, "Why you call Papa Mark, Doc?"

"Habit, I guess. That's what I called him when we first met."

Mark raised an eyebrow. "I thought it was a term of affection."

"That too," Jack replied, chuckling. The phone ringing saved Jack from any further explanation. "Cab's here," he said, hanging up. "Okay, fellas..." He stood, still holding Ghali in his arms. "Time to go…" He put an arm round Mark's shoulders and pulled him close. "Time to go home."

Chapter Seventeen

One year later

The sun was setting behind the mountains when Mark and Jack rode their horses to the edge of the ridge that separated their property from the neighbouring station. A fine rain had fallen recently, bringing the scent of clean grass and leaves to their nostrils.

Mark inhaled then breathed out a long and satisfied sigh. "Beautiful, Jack, isn't it?"

"That it is..." He pulled his mount closer to Mark's and placed a big hand on Mark's thigh. "And you get more beautiful every day." He caressed the muscles beneath his fingers then leant over to kiss Mark's ready lips.

It had been a year of change, of adapting, of challenge for both of them and for the boy they had brought to this still partly untamed land. Out here, far from the bustling city of Brisbane, in this part of the rural heartland, they had cultivated the property Jack's mother had bequeathed him, making it fit for the working horses they now bred and raised. It had been exhausting yet exhilarating, frustrating yet ultimately completely rewarding. Even when Mark's mother and father had arrived unexpectedly to meet the man and the boy Mark had given up everything for. Fortunately, that had gone well, and Ghali now had new grandparents and a home in California to visit in the summer months.

Six months after they had applied for Ghali's permanent residency it had been granted with Jack and Mark appointed his legal guardians. Mark had hoped they could formally adopt Ghali, but in Queensland there was no same-sex adoption law. For that, they'd have to wait, but in the meantime, Ghali's natural high spirits and ability to make friends at the nearby school, proved to them they had made the right decision to bring him to Australia.

They'd had a lot of help and encouragement from Bill Caruthers, Jack's father. A man of few words but with an abiding love for his sons and horses, he had taken Mark and Ghali into his life without hesitation. As a young man, before he'd joined the army, Bill had been a stockman on a huge station that handled upward of thirty thousand cattle. Even then he'd found time to break in some horses, repairing and eventually building saddles, passing these skills onto his sons when they were just boys. It was obvious to Mark that Jack adored his father, a love that was unconditionally returned, and that spilled over to include both Mark and Ghali with its warmth.

Mark had listened to Bill's recollections with rapt attention and admiration. Here was a man who had struggled to find his place in life, but who'd had the courage to rise above his humble beginnings and even propose marriage to a woman, Jack's mother, whom he'd thought would never give him the time of day. Mark could see the same courage and resilience in Jack, and it made him love the man even more.

"Shall we head back home?" he asked, his voice husky with the desire Jack's kiss had brought him. "We have the place all to ourselves tonight, don't forget." Ghali was visiting Bill in Mackay, the coastal town a hundred or so miles from the station. Mark gave Jack the witchy smile he knew always turned his lover to jelly, except that part of him he now couldn't wait to put his hands, and lips, on.

"I hadn't forgotten," Jack said gruffly, pulling on Mark's reins. "Let's go, then. Last one in has to cook dinner after..."

Mark laughed loudly. "What d'you mean? When have I not cooked your dinner?" Still laughing, he urged the bay forward, and together they raced across the verdant meadowland towards home.

After unsaddling their horses and bedding them down for the night, they walked hand in hand to the modest house they had built with the help of Jack's father and brothers. Once inside, Mark lit one of the table lamps. He turned to find Jack watching him, a smile playing on his wide, generous mouth. In the soft glow of the lamp, Jack's sun-darkened skin gleamed with health, vitality and beauty, causing Mark's breath to catch in his throat at the sight.

"What?" he asked softly.

"You," Jack said. "Do I tell you enough how much you mean to me? *Have* meant to me since the day we met in that hell-hole you worked in?" He took the few steps needed to reach Mark and hold him in his embrace. He stifled any reply Mark would have made, pressing his lips to Mark's, his tongue skimming over Mark's lower lip before gently probing, seeking entrance.

Mark's long shuddering sigh from his parted lips filled Jack's mouth with his warm breath. Their arms tightened round one another as their hips moved in a sensual rhythm, grinding their rock hard erections together, inflaming each other with lust and desire.

"God, Jack, I love you…" Mark's mumbled words vibrated on Jack's lips, sending an electric jolt straight to his balls. He groaned, lifted Mark into his arms and headed for their bedroom. "My big butch lover," Mark teased him, pulling at Jack's shirt buttons.

"Lucky you," Jack growled, yanking Mark's shirt over his head without bothering to unbutton it.

They fell on the bed tangled together, tugging impatiently at each other's jeans and boots until they were naked, their hot and eager bodies pressed together in a tumult of passion. Jack's mouth scoured Mark's lips, throat and chest, licking and nibbling his nipples, causing Mark's body to arch and writhe under him, soft moans and whimpers of ecstasy escaping his parted lips.

Jack grasped Mark's hard as steel erection at the base, licking at the glistening head with long swipes of his tongue, before taking it into the moist heat of his mouth. He took all of it, his lips gliding up and down the hard length 'til he sank his nose into the curly blond down at the root. He inhaled Mark's musky scent while his fingers probed the cleft between his lover's buttocks, finding his moist hole, sinking one finger in, then two, finding that sensitive part of him he knew drove Mark mad. Mark's moans grew louder, his hips bucked, driving his cock deep into Jack's mouth, his pre cum spilling down Jack's throat.

"Jack, Jack," Mark gasped, "I'll come if you keep doing that. I want you inside me when I come..."

After a few more sensuous sucks Jack pulled back and lifted Mark's legs, burrowing between them. He teased each of Mark's balls with the tip of his tongue, before licking his way over the silky surface of Mark's perineum. He lost himself in his lover's taste and scent, overwhelming his senses and making him rock hard.

Mark cried out as his eager opening was bathed by Jack's tongue, each flick and probe bringing him ever nearer to the edge of his control. He reached across to the nightstand drawer for the lube, his hand shaking slightly with anticipation. Even though he and Jack had had sex more times than he could remember, the thrill of having his lover inside him never diminished.

"Jack," he whispered, "fuck me..."

Jack raised his head and smiled at him and Mark felt his heart turn over. Jack positioned his powerful body between Mark's thighs and slicked his long thick cock with lube. Mark watched him through eyes heavy lidded with lust and desire. If he lived to be a hundred, he thought he would never tire of looking at Jack's beautifully sculpted body. He lifted himself up to stroke the warm, smooth flesh of Jack's torso, his hands gliding over hard pecs and muscled shoulders. Jack held him with one arm around him while he guided his hot, pulsing cock into Mark's waiting hole. Mark eased himself up onto Jack's lap, taking all he could. He wrapped his arms around Jack's neck, aligning their mouths perfectly, tracing the outline of Jack's lower lip with the tip of his tongue.

Raising his hips slightly, he moved in a circular, sensuous rhythm then bore down hard, taking Jack balls-deep inside him. He gasped into Jack's mouth at the exquisite sensation of being filled by hard flesh buried deep in his velvet heat. Jack's arms tightened around Mark's slim torso, his mouth claiming Mark's in a hot searing kiss that had them both moaning as the intensity of their coupling built to a frantic pitch.

Jack's upward thrusts quickened. His breathing, muffled by Mark's mouth, became ragged and harsh as he neared his climax. He tore his mouth away to cry out Mark's name as he came in violent wrenching spasms, his hot seed flooding Mark's core.

"Jack, oh Jesus, Jack..." Mark shuddered in the bigger man's arms as his orgasm over took him and he clung to Jack as wave after wave of sensual heat coursed through his blood, his cum jetting up between their tightly pressed chests.

Sated and spent, they collapsed onto the mattress, Mark contentedly nuzzling Jack's nipples, Jack tangling his fingers in Mark's thick hair.

"You were fantastic...again," Mark murmured, kissing Jack's chin.

"We're good together, you and me." Jack yawned then kissed Mark's forehead. "Think I need a kip. You're wearing me out."

Mark chuckled. "Like I could. You have your kip then while I fix something to eat."

"Sounds like a plan."

Mark rolled off the bed and smiled down at his already snoozing lover. "Amazing," he muttered. "Wish I could do that."

He pulled on a pair of shorts and walked through to the kitchen. For a moment he paused, looking out the window at the moonlit sky, and not for the first time felt a touch of wonder at just how much his life had changed in the past year. Changed so much for the better; the nightmare of being hunted and kidnapped by crazy men now only a distant memory of a time in a far-off land. Every now and then he would wonder what had happened to the Saudi boys who had taken him along on their plan to escape from Rashid's palace. He could only hope that perhaps Hassan and As'ad had found happiness together despite Jack's prediction their families would never allow it. Maybe they'd run off together once As'ad had recovered — if he'd recovered.

He wished for them the same happiness he had found. Everything he needed — Jack, the man he loved, Ghali, the boy who brought light and laughter into their lives — was right here in this house, on this land he now called home.

He jumped as a warm hard body was pressed to his and soft lips trailed across the nape of his neck. "Thought you were having a kip." He turned in his lover's arms and looked up into the bluest of eyes.

"I got lonesome," Jack murmured. "For you…what were you thinking about?"

"About how much I love being here, in Australia, with you and Ghali."

"Goes for me too." He lowered his head slightly to take Mark's mouth in a long kiss. "You ever goin' to feed me?" he asked when they eventually came up for air.

"Is that all I'm good for?" Mark teased. "Fuckin' and cookin'?"

"Sounds about right," Jack said, grinning, then ducked out of the way as Mark swung at him. He caught Mark's wrist and pulled him into another embrace. "So much more than that," he murmured, holding Mark tightly in his arms. "So much more…"

About the Author

J.P Bowie was born in Scotland and toured British theatres in numerous musical shows including Stephen Sondheim's Company.

Emigrated to the States and worked in Las Vegas, Nevada for the magicians Siegfried and Roy as their Head of Wardrobe at the Mirage Hotel. Currently living in Henderson, Nevada.

J.P. Bowie loves to hear from readers.

You can find his contact information, website details and author profile page at http://www.total-e-bound.com.

Total-E-Bound Publishing

www.total-e-bound.com

Take a look at our exciting range of literagasmic™
erotic romance titles and discover pure quality
at Total-E-Bound.